PURSUED . . .

Carter held the Luger by the barrel, like a club.

The stranger rounded a corner and came face to face with Carter. His right hand shot under his coat.

The first blow caught him in the middle of the forehead. Another nailed him in the back of the head on the way down.

Carter went through his pockets. A credentials case told the story:

"Special Agent J. D. Willis, FBI."

NICK CARTER IS IT!

"Nick Carter out-Bonds James Bond."

—Buffalo Evening News

"Nick Carter is America's #1 espionage agent."

—Variety

"Nick Carter is razor-sharp suspense."

—King Features

"Nick Carter has attracted an army of addicted readers . . . the books are fast, have plenty of action and just the right degree of sex . . . Nick Carter is the American James Bond, suave, sophisticated, a killer with both the ladies and the enemy."

—The New York Times

FROM THE NICK CARTER KILLMASTER SERIES

AFGHAN INTERCEPT
THE ALGARVE AFFAIR
THE ANDROPOV FILE
THE ASSASSIN CONVENTION
ASSIGNMENT: RIO
THE BERLIN TARGET
BLACK SEA BLOODBATH
BLOOD OF THE FALCON
BLOOD OF THE SCIMITAR
BLOOD RAID
BLOOD ULTIMATUM
BLOODTRAIL TO MECCA
THE BLUE ICE AFFAIR
BOLIVIAN HEAT
THE BUDAPEST RUN
CARIBBEAN COUP
CIRCLE OF SCORPIONS
CODE NAME COBRA
COUNTDOWN TO ARMAGEDDON
CROSSFIRE RED
THE CYCLOPS CONSPIRACY
DAY OF THE ASSASSIN
DAY OF THE MAHDI
THE DEADLY DIVA
THE DEATH DEALER
DEATH HAND PLAY
DEATH ISLAND
DEATH ORBIT
DEATH SQUAD
THE DEATH STAR AFFAIR
DEATHSTRIKE
DRAGONFIRE
THE DUBROVNIK MASSACRE
EAST OF HELL
THE EXECUTION EXCHANGE
THE GOLDEN BULL
HOLY WAR
INVITATION TO DEATH
KILLING GAMES
THE KILLING GROUND
THE KREMLIN KILL
LAST FLIGHT TO MOSCOW
THE LAST SAMURAI
LETHAL PREY
THE MACAO MASSACRE
THE MASTER ASSASSIN
THE MAYAN CONNECTION
MERCENARY MOUNTAIN
NIGHT OF THE CONDOR
NIGHT OF THE WARHEADS
THE NORMANDY CODE
NORWEGIAN TYPHOON
OPERATION PETROGRAD
OPERATION SHARKBITE
THE PARISIAN AFFAIR
PRESSURE POINT
THE POSEIDON TARGET
PURSUIT OF THE EAGLE
THE RANGOON MAN
THE REDOLMO AFFAIR
REICH FOUR
RETREAT FOR DEATH
THE SAMURAI KILL
SAN JUAN INFERNO
THE SATAN TRAP
SIGN OF THE COBRA
SLAUGHTER DAY
SOLAR MENACE
SPYKILLER
THE STRONTIUM CODE
THE SUICIDE SEAT
TARGET RED STAR
THE TARLOV CIPHER
TERMS OF VENGEANCE
THE TERROR CODE
TERROR TIMES TWO
TIME CLOCK OF DEATH
TRIPLE CROSS
TUNNEL FOR TRAITORS
TURKISH BLOODBATH
THE VENGEANCE GAME
WAR FROM THE CLOUDS
WHITE DEATH
THE YUKON TARGET
ZERO-HOUR STRIKE FORCE

DAY OF THE ASSASSIN

KILL MASTER

NICK CARTER

J

JOVE BOOKS, NEW YORK

KILLMASTER #247: DAY OF THE ASSASSIN

A Jove Book / published by arrangement with
The Condé Nast Publications, Inc.

PRINTING HISTORY
Jove edition / March 1989

ISBN: 0-515-09958-9

Jove Books are published by The Berkley Publishing Group,
200 Madison Avenue, New York, New York 10016.

PRINTED IN THE UNITED STATES OF AMERICA

10 9 8 7 6 5 4 3 2 1

Dedicated to the men and women of the
Secret Services of the
United States of America

ONE

Herb Lawson carried three hundred and seventy pounds on a six-foot frame. A good hunk of that weight was in the ponderous belly that hung over his gun belt. He had stringy black hair, watery eyes, and a nervous tic at the corner of his mouth.

But when Herb looked in a mirror, which he did often, he didn't see an overweight, worn-out Podunk sheriff. He saw the Lone Ranger.

Lawson had been sheriff of Modesto County for seventeen years and had never arrested anything bigger than a hubcap thief.

But all that had changed in the last twelve hours with the arrest of Jack Kirby.

Sheriff Lawson didn't really know what the FBI wanted with Kirby, and he didn't care. The fact that the Bureau had a "most wanted" out on the man, and Lawson had captured him, was enough.

His place in the law-enforcement sun was made. There would be no more snide jokes around Beeson about old Herb Lawson being the "fat, dumb, and happy sheriff of Modesto County."

It didn't matter that Jack Kirby had fallen asleep and

ran off the road just outside Beeson. Lawson had already forgotten that aspect of the arrest. In the new version, he and his deputy, Lonnie Kinkaid, had "thrown down" the suspect after a high-speed chase. Lawson himself had faced him out, eyeball to eyeball, and Kirby had surrendered rather than face the sheriff's lightning draw.

"Clint Eastwood or the Duke hisself couldn't'a done it no better," Lawson told himself.

"Sheriff?"

"Yeah, Lonnie?"

Lonnie Kinkaid was twenty-one and as thin as Lawson was heavy. Until Sheriff Lawson had taken him on as his deputy, Lonnie had been the night pearl diver at Sam's Diner across the street from the jail.

The good citizens of Beeson had been a little surprised when Lonnie was hired. The boy had never been too bright. It was a known fact that Lonnie had failed the written test to get into the Army.

Sheriff Lawson had calmed everybody down by explaining that, by working for the minimum wage and buying his own uniform, Lonnie would save the taxpayers money. The people of Beeson were further assured when they learned that Lonnie would be issued no bullets for his gun.

"Sheriff, Marvin threw up in his cell again."

Lawson sighed. "Well, give him a pail and a mop. Tell the som'bitch to clean it up hisself."

"Yessir. An' that Kirby feller is beggin' like hell fer ya to send a message fer him."

Lawson hooted. "Probably to the CIA. That som'bitch is rowin' with one oar, I tell ya."

"Yessir."

Lonnie meandered into the cell area, and Sam came through the front door.

"Got the prisoners' supper, Sheriff."

"Jes' set it there, Sam. I'll take it back."

"Boy, town's sure proud, Sheriff. Hear you catched a real desperado an' the FBI is comin' to get him. Hot damn!"

"Jes' police work, Sam. Here ya go."

The man left with the signed chit, and Lawson lifted the corner of a cloth covering one of the trays. Supper consisted of chicken-fried steak, dumplings and gravy, greens, and Jell-O.

"Som'bitchin' prisoners eat better'n I do," he grumbled under his breath.

Carrying the trays, he unlocked the door into the cell block and entered.

The interior of the small block was dim, illuminated by two bare bulbs in the hall and one in each of the three cells.

In the first cell, the town drunk, Marvin Cox, was listlessly mopping up the pail of water he had just kicked over. In the third cell, a tall, athletically built man in his early twenties leaned against the barred door and watched the sheriff approach.

"Supper, Kirby."

"That's nice, but I don't want any."

"Suit yerself."

Kirby's hands gripped the bars until his knuckles were white. "I know you think I'm crazy, Sheriff . . ."

"Hell, no, son, I think you're damn smart. I mean, hell, there ain't many fugitives who'd rig themselves up with CIA credentials to escape capture!"

"Sheriff, I am a special agent."

"Sure ya are!" Lawson said, laughing. "The FBI puts out wanteds on CIA agents all the time!"

"That 'wanted' didn't come from the FBI," Kirby said in frustration. "I tried to explain this to you before. They've tapped into telex lines, into the computers. Hell, they can put out a 'want' on anybody in the country with just a keyboard and a phone line."

"Sure, Kirby. Who's 'they'?"

"I can't tell you that."

"Then you can tell the FBI. They'll be pickin' you up in about a half hour."

Lawson set the tray on the floor in front of the pass-through hole in the door. He started for the door.

"Sheriff, at least send a message for me . . ."

Lawson paused. "What kind of message?" He thought he'd better listen. The FBI might be able to use the information.

"Here, I'll write in on the napkin. This is important, Sheriff. Let me use your pen."

Kirby scrawled on the napkin and handed it and the pen back to Lawson.

Arnold Pierce, c/o Del Rey Beach and Tennis Club, Marina del Rey, Calif. Plot is phony. You are the patsy. Pull out. Kirby.

"Please, Sheriff, send this telegram at once. It's a matter of national security . . . Sheriff . . . Sheriff—"

Lawson shut the cell-block door behind him, cutting off Kirby's voice.

"What did he want?" Lonnie asked.

"Send a wire to Marina del Rey."

"Hmmm, prob'ly his confederates in crime."

"Prob'ly," Lawson said. "What're you doin'?"

"Eatin' Marvin's dinner. Hell, he's got too much Thunderbird in him to hold it down. No sense lettin' it go to waste."

The sound of a car pulling to the curb outside caught both men's attention. Lonnie stood and walked to the window.

"Hot damn, sure looks lke the FBI! They's wearin' suits and they's got a steely glint in their eyes!"

"Lonnie, you're watchin' too much TV."

Two men stepped into the office. Even in their suits, crisp white shirts, and ties, the outside heat didn't seem to have affected them. The taller of the two spoke.

"Sheriff Lawson?"

"I'm Lawson."

The taller man slipped a leather credentials case from his jacket and dropped it open. The shorter one followed suit.

"Special Agent Wynne," he said. "And this is my partner, Agent Cruz."

Cruz nodded politely. "Sheriff."

Lawson looked over the contents of both credential cases very carefully, as if he were reading every word and fold. Actually, he looked at just the names and the FBI seal. It was the first FBI identification he had ever seen.

"Looks fine," he said, and took a form from his desk drawer and handed it to Wynne. "Just sign this release and he's all yours."

"Has he tried to make contact with anyone?" the tall man asked, scratching the form with a pen.

"Not really," Lawson replied.

"Wanted the sheriff to send a wire," the deputy interjected.

"Oh, yeah." Lawson pulled the crumpled napkin from his pocket and passed it to Wynne.

"We'll follow this up," Wynne said, exchanging a look and a nod with his partner. "If it's all right with you we'll take him now."

"Sure thing," Lawson said, moving to the cell-block door. "Guess you know he claims to be a CIA man. I ran his name through Washington and came up with bullshit, of course."

The sheriff and his deputy moved into the cell block.

The two agents paused in the doorway, their images blurred by the backlighting from the office.

In the cell, Kirby jumped to his feet. "Oh, my God! No, Sheriff—"

From the doorway there was a dull, thumping sound. Lonnie grunted and flew forward, his arms outstretched.

Lawson caught the deputy in his arms. At the same time, he saw cause and effect. Half of the back of Lonnie's head was a bloody mess and the two FBI agents had silenced automatics in their hands.

"Som'bitch!" Lawson cried, his hand dropping toward the police special at his belt.

He never made it.

Wynne's automatic thumped again. The bullet split Lawson's forehead, killing him instantly and sending his body reeling backward into the bars of Kirby's cell.

The prisoner jammed his arm through the bars, trying to reach the sheriff's gun. Both automatics barked at once, stitching a neat six-shot pattern in the center of Kirby's chest. He staggered backward, dead before he fell across the cell's cot.

In cell number one, Marvin Cox came off his cot and stared bleary-eyed at the carnage.

"What the hell's goin' on?" he muttered thickly.

Cruz aimed his automatic through the bars and shot Cox twice.

Wynne checked each of the bodies and nodded to Cruz. Both men unscrewed the silencers from their guns, slipped them into their pockets, holstered the guns, then walked across the office and out the front door.

TWO

The Potomac Club on Harris Boulevard in Arlington was *the* watering hole for the poorer class of Washington journalist. If you were a scribe with a small expense account, or, worse yet, a free-lancer with *no* expense account, the Potomac was the place to wash away the day's grime from a parched throat.

On the midweek night, every stool at the bar was full and there were stragglers at about a third of the tables.

Sitting close at a table near the end of the bar was a tall, rather willowy woman dressed in a severe gray tweed suit. Even bloodshot, her pale blue eyes were astonishingly alert. At one time, perhaps only a few years past, she was probably a striking woman. Now, in her late thirties, she looked worn and used.

Suddenly her head came up from her chest and the glass she held slammed the table. "You're talking about me again! I heard you! Which one of you is knifing me in the back now?"

At the bar, tired newsmen looked at each other through weary, slightly bulging eyes, and nodded.

Cory Reader had a snootful again.

"Knock it off! I'm telling ya . . ." Cory stood unsteadily and, waving her glass in one hand, staggered to the bar. The men turned away from her gin breath and the heavy scent of her perfume.

No one answered her. No one ever answered her. The hubbub in the bar dropped momentarily and then rose again.

Unaccountably, Cory began to sob.

Immediately around her there lay an awkward, constricted pool of silence. These men knew her. When Cory was loaded she was always like this. There was nothing that could be done.

"Nobody cares," she moaned.

Masculine feet shifted heavily, uncomfortably. Tired eyes sought tired wristwatches. Wives would be surprised to have their husbands home early tonight.

"Nobody cares!"

Nobody had cared about Cory Reader in a long, long time. Nobody had cared since Cory herself stopped caring, since the day she exchanged the humdrum homespun of friendship for the bright and brilliant bauble of success.

She had come into Washington a "nice girl." They were mostly like that when they first reached the city. It was only later that some of them became ruthlessly ambitious, and wanted success for its own sake.

She had been one of those.

She had seen success as a thing to be desired above all else. She had been dazzled by it. She had seen it as a thing to lie and to cheat for. She had climbed high, far, and fast in the newsprint jungle. The rungs of her ladder had been dashed promises, discarded friendships, and the broken lives of her enemies.

She had been something to look at then, something to draw a swift, sharp breath about.

Nothing had been sacred to her in her quest for the brilliant bauble. She would sacrifice anything or anyone in the battle to reach her objective. She had stormed success, captured it by reason of her sex and ruthless, driving determination.

No one else had been surprised to see it fracture, all too quickly, in her hands.

She had made so many enemies on the way up, sharpened so many long, thin knives for unsuspecting backs, that this remained a habit with her after she had arrived.

She did not reign long.

A few had loved her, but no one liked her. She had no friends. She began to slip, and others, just as ruthless as she, helped her on her way . . . down. She ceased to be successful. She became a rung on someone else's ladder. She plummeted, and there was nothing to break her fall.

After that, Cory Reader lost interest in almost everything. Everything except the haunting memory of the success she had briefly enjoyed in the past, and the prospect of making a comeback in the future.

She could talk of nothing else, think of nothing else. Her hair grew long and lank, like wet straw. Her breasts drooped. Her body grew slack. She didn't care. Her mind was fevered.

She'd make a comeback! She'd scale those heights again! She'd show them!

She lived on pity and charity—on free-lance assignments given her by ex-lovers, and editors who told themselves that they ought to know better. She accepted the work offered in a manner that suggested it was she who was conferring the favor, and she turned in her copy—when she was not too drunk to write it—and it was almost always bad.

Almost always, but, strangely, not invariably.

Occasionally, very occasionally, her copy would seem to be lit from within by some hard and brilliant fire. Then editors, surprised, might even give her a byline. But, normally, her work was deadly stuff: stale, and flat, and unusable. Whichever it was, it was paid for.

It was paid so that she might live; so that she might drink; so that she might create harrowing scenes in pubs all over the city.

It was paid for so that she might be able to cry paradoxically, "Nobody cares!"

A young reporter fumbled a twenty into her hand. "I'll get you a cab, Cory. You go home."

She whirled on him, her eyes flashing. "Keep your money! I don't want it! Keep it!"

He wouldn't take it back, and she threw it on the floor. She trampled on it in sudden rage. "Putrid, rotten men!"

"Now . . . Cory . . ." A waitress was standing beside her. "Cory—"

"Take your hands off me! Leave me alone!" Her cheeks were splotched with scarlet. "Don't touch me!" She began to weave a pathetically dignified path to the door. "I'll go, I'll go. I know I'm not wanted. I don't have to stay here."

The young reporter had picked up his twenty. He tried again. "Get a cab . . ."

She brushed his hand away. "I don't want your damned charity." Her head went back. "I don't need it. I'm making my own way. Up to the top, d'ya hear? Up to the top!" She swayed precariously, addressing the room in general. "You think I'm finished, don't you? You all think I'm finished . . ."

Her mouth fell slackly open. She tasted bile. She made a sweeping gesture that nearly overbalanced her.

"Scribblers!" she sneered with contempt. "Hacks, all of you!"

They looked at her, not saying anything, and their eyes were more tired than ever.

Cory's voice rose high and shrill. "I'm not finished. Not by a long shot! I'm going to be rich, d'ya hear? Rich! More money than you miserable hacks have ever dreamed of!"

They didn't answer. Nobody answered her.

Nobody cared.

Her face desolate, she suddenly swung away from them and stumbled out into the street.

As she bounced her shoulder off the sides of buildings, she fumbled in her purse for a cigarette.

"Oh, damn . . ."

Her eye had fallen on the thick white envelope. She had forgotten to mail it. She had put the stamps on it and carefully addressed it just the way he had instructed, and then she had forgotten to mail the damn thing.

She squinted her eyes down the dimly lit street. Two blocks away, on the other side of the street, she spotted the familiar blue of a mailbox.

She staggered off.

A block behind her, an older model Ford LTD idled along close to the curb.

Directly across from the box, Cory paused. She pulled the envelope from her bag and lurched into the street.

The car was only a few feet from her when Cory heard its screaming engine. The impact threw her over a hundred feet. She was dead when she hit the pavement and the Ford rocked to a halt beside her.

The driver, a tall, handsome young man in a dark pin-striped suit, was out of the car in an instant. Deftly, with practiced fingers, he went through her pockets and then her purse. Finding nothing of interest, he pried the envelope from her fingers and read the address: *Arnold Pierce, c/o Del Rey Beach and Tennis Club, Marina del Rey, California.*

Scrawled across the bottom was, *Hold for Pick-up.*

He jammed the envelope into his pocket and jumped back in the car.

THREE

Horst's served the best German food in the whole Baltimore-Washington area. It was also an easy three-block walk from Nick Carter's Georgetown digs. Always, when he was in Washington between assignments, Carter would dine at least twice weekly at Horst's.

He was just sliding into his favorite booth when the owner, Horst Binsdorfer, came charging over. Binsdorfer had come over the Wall from East Berlin ten years earlier. Carter had been helpful in getting him out, and the old man had never forgotten it.

"Nick, you look good!"

"Horst, the same. Sit."

The German slid into the booth and leaned forward conspiratorially. "You chasing any women with jealous husbands lately?"

Carter smiled. "I don't think so. Why?"

The restaurateur slid a thin envelope across the table. "A gorgeous blonde left this for you the day before yesterday. She said to give it only to you. She seemed to know that we're friends."

The envelope was tightly sealed. Carter tore off the

end and shook out a single sheet of note paper: *Nick, please contact me in N.Y. (212) 555-7177. Very, very important. Trilby Royce.*

Carter screwed his face in concentration. He remembered a tall, gangling girl of about fourteen, with braces, a long braid, and narrow-minded ideas on how people like Carter and her father, Josh Royce, were polluting the world with their cloak-and-dagger crap.

"Important?"

"I don't know, Horst. Can I use your office phone?"

"Sure."

Horst escorted Carter to his office above the restaurant and discreetly left him alone.

The number rang five times before a sleepy voice answered in a thick accent.

"Could I speak to Trilby Royce, please?"

"Trilby Royce? You must have the wrong number."

"Is this 555-7177?"

"Yes, but there is no one here by that name."

"That's odd. I got a message . . ."

"But I am Helga. Perhaps you'd like to talk to me? What's your name . . . you have a nice voice . . ."

"The name is Nick and I'm sorry I disturbed you."

He hung up and returned to the table. He was halfway through a mountainous portion of sauerbrauten and red cabbage when the head waiter appeared at his elbow.

"Mr. Carter?"

"Yes?"

"Telephone call, sir. Herr Binsdorfer says you can take it in his office."

"Thanks."

He made the trek through the tables a second time, and closed the office door behind him.

"Carter here."

"Nick, this is Trilby Royce. Sorry about the little

runaround. I wasn't here when you called."

"Who was the bunny on the phone?"

"That was Helga. She shares this apartment with two other stewardesses. I'm just crashing. Nick, I need to see you."

"Okay, how about lunch tomorrow?"

"How about drinks tonight."

"Tonight?"

"Please, Nick, grab the next shuttle. It's important."

Carter mulled this over for a few seconds. "Does this have anything to do with your father?"

"Yes. Will you come . . . tonight?"

He checked his watch. "I'll see you in a couple of hours."

"Wonderful," she said, obvious relief in her voice. "And, Nick . . . do you have to let anyone know you're coming?"

"Afraid so."

"Do you have to let them know who you're meeting?"

"No," he replied, "that doesn't have to be a part of it."

"Good." She gave him a Riverside Drive address. "It's six-B. Please hurry, Nick. I'm scared to death."

She hung up and Carter stood staring at the instrument in his hand.

Now, he thought, *what the hell had Josh Royce gotten himself into?*

Josh Royce was a dog soldier, the meanest of the mean. After fifteen years of Army life he had resigned his commission and joined the Company. In the twenty years he'd been with the CIA, Carter had worked with him often.

Royce was violently patriotic, gung-ho, without nerves, and a good man to have at your back.

If he had a fault, it was in the extremes of his thinking. For Josh Royce there was no gray, only black and white. More often than not, this had landed him in hot water with his cooler-headed superiors who were forced to see all sides of a question.

Carter hadn't seen Royce for nearly seven years. In that time he had heard that Royce had retired and taken some cushy job in private industry.

As the taxi drove through Queens from La Guardia into Manhattan, the Killmaster found himself growing more and more uneasy.

Josh Royce had never been a paragon. In the past, he had often pushed the rules to the breaking point, and risked lives and the success of a mission in the process. Now, working in the private sector, his cowboy ways were probably a lot worse.

And the daughter, Trilby, how was she involved?

"Here ya are, chief. Eighteen-fifty."

Carter passed a twenty and a ten through the bulletproof shield that protected the driver from his fellow men, and stepped from the cab.

He took a tiny elevator to the sixth floor and rang the bell beside 6B. When it wasn't answered, he checked the crack under the door and saw a light. He rang again and the light went out.

"Damn," he growled. He put his finger on the button and left it there. In about ninety seconds, somebody fumbled with the knob and the door opened a crack, as far as the chain bolt would let it.

"Who is it?"

"The Sultan of Oman, for God's sake, Trilby."

"Nick?"

"The last time I looked in a mirror. Open the door, kid, before I walk through the wood."

The door opened into a darkened hallway. Carter entered and it slammed behind him. He heard a half-dozen locks click and chains drop into place before she took his arm.

"This way."

The living room was nearly as dim until she snapped on a lamp. The room wasn't large, but it was impressive, like the greeting room of a turn-of-the-century whorehouse might be impressive.

Where there wasn't gaudy red-flocked velvet there were mirrors, dozens of them. Most of the furniture consisted of cushions on the floor. The few chairs were tufted in scarlet and gold. The carpet was deep red pile and the ceiling was full of stars.

"Interesting place," Carter commented dryly.

"It belongs to one of Helga's rich boyfriends. He's a little kinky."

Carter turned and got his first good look at the grown-up Trilby Royce.

She was tall and deeply tanned, with a body that did wonderful things to a pair of stone-washed jeans and a lightweight sweater. Under a wealth of dark blond hair she had strong features, an arched nose, unplucked brows, and full lips.

"Something wrong?"

"Not really," he said with a grin. "Just give me a chance to get used to the lack of braces and braids."

She managed the hint of a smile. "That was eleven years ago, Nick. I'm twenty-five now, all grown up."

"I can see that."

"Would you like a drink?"

"I could be talked into it. Scotch, neat."

He had sensed her nervousness the moment he had entered the room. Now he could see it. Her hands as she poured the drinks shook visibly. Eventually she got a gin and tonic built for herself and some scotch poured.

There was one sofa, a horrible peppermint-striped job. They sat on this. Trilby curled her legs under her and Carter lit a cigarette.

"Thanks for coming."

"No problem," he said, tasting the scotch. "Tell me about the grown-up Trilby Royce."

She shrugged. "Nothing too spectacular. Graduated from Stanford. Went on to Harvard for an M.B.A. I've been out in the cold, cruel world of business for nearly two years. Most of that time as an analyst for the *International Business Review*."

"I'm impressed," he said, and paused to study her darting eyes over the rim of his glass. "How's your father?"

Her head jerked up as if he had reached out and pinched her. Then she heaved a deep sigh.

"Up to his ass in alligators, as usual."

"I assume that was why you chased me down at Horst's?"

She nodded. "Josh said it was the only way to reach you outside the agency."

Carter sighed. It was about what he had expected. If Royce didn't want anyone in State, the CIA, or any other agency to know he was trying to reach Carter, then the old agent was in something shady up to his eyeballs.

"Suppose, Trilby, you start at the top."

Abruptly, she uncurled her long legs and planted her feet on the floor. "You knew Josh retired from the Company?"

"Yes. I heard he got a pretty good private-sector job."

"Partially true. He's still listed as a consultant. That gives him some access at Langley. He went to work for Comrex."

A little tickle ran up Carter's spine. "A private, nonprofit corporation headquartered in Bern, Switzerland.

The company's primary objective is to fight the spread of worldwide Communism through aid to right-wing factions, generally in Third World countries."

She was surprised. "You know about Comrex?"

"Not much," Carter admitted. "Like so many others of the same ilk, they landed on our 'watch' list. It's the kind of outfit your father would get involved with."

"Yeah," she said dryly, "how well I know. For the first two years he worked for them, he was hopping all over the world. I hardly saw him. Of course, that was nothing new; I hardly saw him my whole life. Then, about three months ago, he pops up at my apartment in Boston and wants me to do some research for him."

"On Comrex?"

"Yes," she replied.

"Let me get this straight. Josh wanted you to dig into the company he was working for?"

"Right again," she said. "It seems one of his old girlfriends, a newspaperwoman named Cory Reader, had come to him with some statistical dirt which was TNT."

Carter eyed his empty glass and decided to freshen it himself. "Such as?"

"Comrex had no visible means of support or income. Yet they have amassed millions. They have also recruited what amounts to a global underground army."

Carter returned to the sofa. "That's really nothing new, Trilby. There are radical groups all over the world."

"Maybe so," she said, nodding, "but not with Comrex's ambitions. I did an in-depth study to find out Comrex's sources of funds and where the money is going. Nick, some of the most powerful men in the world have put vast sums at Comrex's disposal. A big chunk of that money has been funneled into Africa. I found out that two small countries are already in Comrex's pocket. They were literally bought and paid for."

Carter pondered this for a few moments. "What was Josh's reaction when you gave him this information?"

"He intimated that it was about what he had expected. He took all my findings and passed them on to Cory Reader. He seemed to think that with my information she could uncover the Comrex chain of command and the top man."

"And . . . ?" Carter asked.

"Evidently she was getting pretty close, close enough for my father to take what he had to his old superiors in the Company."

"Go on."

"He was waiting for an answer in a Baltimore hotel, when three men tried to kill him. He recognized one of them as Phillip Walker. Nick, Phil Walker is still in the Company, very well placed, section chief in Lisbon."

"So Comrex has fingers inside the Company?"

She nodded. "Josh has been on the run ever since. Three nights ago, I returned to my Boston apartment. It was a shambles. All my files had been taken, even those on Comrex. Thankfully, I had everything on Comrex duplicated on microfilm." She held up her handbag. "It's all in here."

Carter lit a cigarette, the newly poured scotch forgotten for the moment. "What does Josh think? I mean, what is Comrex's ultimate goal?"

"Don't laugh," Trilby said, her jaw set, her eyes unwavering as they met his. "They are opting for the control of southern and central Africa."

"What?"

"Think about it, Nick. There is a lot of chaos in all the decolonized countries. There's no strong, central leadership, and what leadership there is, is corrupt or just downright ineffectual. With enough power, organization, and money . . ." She paused, shrugging.

Now Carter took the drink, in two long swallows. What Trilby said made sense. It was the divide-and-conquer form of revolution so popular with the Communists, only in reverse. With the proper staging area for small revolutionary armies, and enough propaganda money, anything would be possible in strife- and poverty-ridden countries.

"Where is Josh now?"

"On the run, but now he has help . . . or *had* help."

"What does that mean?"

"He convinced two of his old friends in the Company to help him, Jack Kirby and Vince D'Ambrosio. They've been working from the inside."

Here she paused, tugging a newspaper clipping from her purse. Carter took it and read.

"So much for Jack Kirby. Beeson is a little out of the way. Where do you think he was headed?"

"We were all going to meet in Marina del Rey, day after tomorrow, at the Del Rey Beach and Tennis Club."

"Why there?"

"Josh didn't say, other than he thought it would be safe."

"Where's D'Ambrosio?" Carter asked.

"According to Josh, he hasn't made contact for three days. That's why Josh told me to contact you. He needs help from the inside. Will you help, Nick?"

Carter stood and moved to the window. This was out of his line, way out. But it was something that David Hawk, the chief of AXE, would probably give him a green light for, at least on the exploratory level.

He made his decision.

"I know a place in the Village where I can take a quick gander at the microfilm you've got. I can also make a couple of phone calls from there. If the man says okay, I'll go."

Trilby hesitated. "Josh says they have lines into everywhere."

Carter smiled, thinking of David Hawk and AXE security. "Believe me, honey, they don't have lines to the man I answer to."

She shrugged and grabbed the bag. "Okay, Josh says you're the only one left he can trust."

They were headed for the door when it opened and a leggy blonde sauntered into the room. She wore a white knit dress that looked as if it had been sprayed onto her perfect body. Her hair was pale blond and hung straight to her shoulders, long bangs framing a face beaming with interest as she gave Carter a once-over.

"Helga, this is Nick."

"Ah, the sexy voice! A little mean-looking, but cute!"

Carter shook her hand and smiled. "Nice to meet you, Helga."

Trilby gave her a brief hug. "I'm packed," she said. "I'll probably be leaving later. Thanks for everything."

"It's fine, anytime," the girl replied, and flashed her version of a scorching look at Carter. "The next time you visit Trilby, bring a friend."

"I'll do that."

On the way to the elevator, Trilby slid her arm through Carter's. "Helga likes men," she chuckled.

"I would have never guessed."

Twenty minutes later, Carter was bent over a mini-projector studying the research that Trilby Royce had gathered. It didn't take long to see what Josh Royce had already realized.

FOUR

In Southern California it rains only two or three weeks a year. And when it does, it isn't just a shower, it's a deluge.

Standing beneath the canopy of the Chinese restaurant, Josh Royce didn't mind the rain. The absence of traffic and pedestrians made it easier for him to spot a tail.

In the last three hours he had gone from downtown Los Angeles to Santa Monica to the Valley and back downtown. This had been accomplished using four taxi cabs and a lot of shoe leather. Now he was in Chinatown and ready to make contact.

Somewhere in his late fifties, Josh Royce stood erect, his firm, hard-muscled body contained perfectly in a conservative business suit and a damp Burberry trench coat. So perfectly did his garments fit that, combined with the way he stood, they seemed to be a uniform.

His face was firmly chiseled and flawless, except for a scar that reached from just under the top of his left cheekbone down to the corner of a mouth which now sported a sardonic grin. A jutting jaw, small pointed ears, and light blue humorless eyes completed the portrait.

Sure now that he wasn't being followed, Royce tugged his collar up and bent forward into the rain.

It took him a half hour to reach the downtown end of Alvarado and the Augustine Hotel. It was one of those half-residential, half-transient buildings that settled in at about forty bucks a week above a fleabag.

The lobby had once been elegant. Now the drapes, leather furniture, and carpet were faded and worn. It was after ten, so the aged night clerk had already disappeared into his cubicle behind the mail slots to sleep away the last eight hours of his shift.

The room was on the fourth floor. Royce rode up in a lumbering old elevator and found 410 at the far end of the first cross corridor.

He rapped gently on the door three times and waited. When there was no reply, he pulled a magnum from the right-hand pocket of the Burberry and tried the knob.

The door was unlocked.

Slowly he pushed it open.

"Vince . . ."

No answer.

He moved into the center of the sitting room and stood listening. The television was on without sound. In its light he could see into a tiny kitchenette. It was empty.

Gently he pushed open the bedroom door. Across the room a light was on in the bath. Vince D'Ambrosio was sprawled facedown, half in the bathroom, half in the bedroom.

Royce laid one finger on the side of his friend's neck. There wasn't even a flicker of a pulse and the flesh was already spongy. D'Ambrosio had been dead for a good two hours, maybe more.

Royce rolled him over, took one look, and said, "Shit, you poor bastard."

Vince D'Ambrosio had been shot in both kneecaps with something small, probably a .22 or a .25. Evidently he still hadn't talked, so they had nailed him one more place before putting the coup de grace slug between his eyes.

Hemingway's Jake Barnes had said it in *The Sun Also Rises:* "It was a rotten way to be wounded."

Royce went through D'Ambrosio's pockets. Nothing, not even loose change. The rest of the room was the same. Other than the body itself, there was no sign that anybody had ever been there.

Royce stood in the center of the room and thought out his next move.

First Jack Kirby and now Vince D'Ambrosio. They didn't have to tail him. All they had to do was wait until he showed up to make the contact. The Del Rey Beach and Tennis Club was out now, but he would have to get word to Trilby.

He slipped the magnum back into his trench coat pocket and took the elevator back down to the lobby. Boldly he walked out the front door and paused to light a small cigar on the stoop.

He knew they were watching from somewhere now.

The hell with it, he thought, they knew where he was going. He would just have to lose them when he got there.

Wynne, now dressed in work clothes, stood in a darkened phone booth three blocks from the hotel. He wore blue jeans, a dark long-sleeved pullover, a windbreaker, and jogging shoes. In the pocket of the windbreaker was a ski mask. In his belt under the windbreaker was a .22 revolver rigged with a silencer.

On the street a half block away, Special Agent Cruz sat in a battered Ford. He was dressed exactly like Wynne.

Both of them watched Royce light his cigar and walk up the street into the darkness. After about two blocks, Royce hopped into a cruising cab.

Wynne dropped a coin into the phone and dialed "O" and then a number in Washington, D.C.

"May I halp you?"

"Yes, Operator, I want to make this a collect call. My name is Wynne."

The other end answered. "Comrex."

"I have a collect call from Mr. Wynne. Will you accept?"

"Yes, Operator."

"Go ahead."

Wynne waited until the operator was off the line before he spoke. "Patch me through."

There was a series of clicks and a second phone was answered with a grunt.

"Wynne, General."

"Yes, son, how did it go?"

"D'Ambrosio is canceled. Our bird is on the wing again."

"Good, good. Just make sure he keeps flying in the right direction. The newspaper connection has also been eliminated."

Wynne chuckled. "Then that leaves only the girl."

"That is being looked into."

The line went dead. Wynne hung up and headed for the Ford.

"Marina del Rey?" Cruz asked when his partner was in the passenger seat.

"Marina del Rey," Wynne replied with a nod.

FIVE

Beside him in the rear seat of the taxi returning to the Riverside Drive apartment, Trilby Royce was silent but calm. The tension Carter had seen in the cab going downtown had disappeared as a result of his phone call to Washington.

The founder and director of AXE, David Hawk, was secluded in Maine for his annual ulcer-relieving fishing trip. His next-in-command, a very bright sable-haired beauty from Atlanta, Ginger Batemen, had been skeptical. That is, until Carter had voiced a consensus of Josh and Trilby Royce's findings. When the Killmaster had added his own gut feelings, Ginger had agreed that it was worth looking into.

"I'll have Research pick it up on this end," she had said. "Have Marc make copies of what you have and courier them down to me right away."

"No need," Carter replied. "I've got everything pertinent from them in my head. I'll send down the originals."

"Good enough. Keep in touch as soon as you contact Royce."

Reading the tone in Batemen's voice told Carter what he already knew. She and informed AXE personnel didn't have a great deal of respect for Josh Royce. Like Carter, AXE headquarters had run afoul of Royce's cowboy methods on several occasions.

Carter set up times to report back to Washington, and instructed Marc Juniper, the audio-visual free-lancer, where and how to send the microfilm. Then he and Trilby had found the cab.

"Right here is fine," Carter said, leaning forward in the seat.

Trilby threw him a sharp glance but said nothing. Carter had instructed the driver to stop a good six blocks from the building housing Helga's boyfriend's apartment.

Carter paid off the driver and they walked in a long arc around several blocks.

"We're being followed?"

"I haven't spotted a tail," Carter growled, "but I've got a tickle in my backside. My tickles usually mean something."

Trilby had her key ready when they reached the door. Inside, they heard the shower running in the bedroom to the right.

"I'll tell Helga it's us." Trilby moved into the bedroom. "Nick . . . !"

Carter took two seconds to answer the shout.

In the bedroom Trilby was looking down at Helga. The stewardess was on her back on one side of the bed. Panty hose bound her wrists and ankles securely to the head and foot boards.

Her eyes were round and wide with fear. She was nude, and gurgling sounds came through the washcloth stuffed in her mouth.

"Brandy," Carter hissed to Trilby, and removed the gag.

As she gulped air into her lungs, Carter untied the panty hose from her wrists and ankles and helped her to a sitting position. He pulled the sheet free and she clutched it to her chin.

"The son of a bitch! I was in the shower!" she gasped. "I didn't hear him come in over the noise of the water. The first thing I know, he's got an arm around my neck and he's dragging me out here to the bed!"

Trilby returned with the brandy. Helga took it, letting the sheet fall, then tried to hold it while she drank and shook. Eventually she just let the sheet bunch in her lap and held the brandy in both hands.

"How did it happen?" Trilby asked.

Helga shivered and cursed again. "I don't know how he got in. I didn't hear anything in the shower. It all happened so fast. Can I have some more brandy?"

Trilby took the glass. Carter went out and examined the hall door chain and the outside lock. There were minuscule scratches around the key slot in the brass. He went into the bath and shut off the shower.

Back in the bedroom, Trilby was sitting beside Helga. Her story was simple. The telephone had rung shortly after Carter and Trilby had left. It was a wrong number. She started to lock the chain, and remembered that they were returning. She undressed, and was in the shower when an arm suddenly reached through the curtain and dragged her, wet and protesting into the bedroom.

"God, he was strong . . . and big!"

"Bigger than I am?" Carter asked.

"*Ja*, maybe three inches taller, and heavier. But he wasn't fat. I grabbed his arm. It was like steel."

"Did you get a look at his face?"

"No. He wore a mask, like skiers wear."

"What color were his eyes?"

Helga snapped her fingers. "Blue. I didn't think I would notice, but I remember. They were a real light, almost opaque, blue."

Trilby stood. "I'm going to check the other bedroom."

She left and Carter straddled a chair beside the bed. He lit a cigarette and offered Helga the pack.

She shook her head. "I don't smoke. God, I thought he was a rapist, until he asked about you."

"Me?"

She nodded. "He wanted to know everything . . . your name, when you got here, where you and Trilby went . . ."

"Did you tell him?"

She swallowed, hard. "Sorry. I was scared."

"No problem," Carter said. "Try to remember anything else about him. Did you see his hair at all?"

"No."

"Cologne, after shave?"

"I don't remember."

"What kind of a voice did he have?"

"Low, almost pleasing, very proper. Oh, my God . . ."

"What?" Carter asked.

"From the shower to the bed, he spoke English. I was cursing him in German. After he tied me up and started questioning me, he spoke German, good German, like a Berliner."

Carter stood and squeezed her shoulder. "That'll help."

He crossed the hall into the other bedroom. There was an open bag on the bed. Clothes and manuscript paper littered the floor. The bathroom was a mess. Whoever the man was, he knew how to search a place and do it fast. Even the top had been pulled off the toilet tank and tossed carelessly into the tub.

Trilby was leaning against a table edge, her arms crossed under her breasts. "Sloppy, wasn't he?" she said bitterly.

"Anything missing?"

"I don't think so." Her toe nudged the broken portable typewriter on the floor. The keys had been stomped on and the carriage pried loose. "I was sure no one had followed me here from Boston."

Suddenly she was trembling. Carter slid his arms around her waist and tugged. She curled into him willingly.

"Don't blame yourself. Whoever these guys are, they're thorough and they've got numbers. We're going to have to do some fancy footwork."

"What now?"

"Repack your bag. I'm making some phone calls."

He moved into the living room, built a light scotch, and attacked a phone. Two calls got him the next five flights out of Kennedy for various destinations.

The third call was to Marc Juniper.

"Jesus, Carter, don't you ever sleep?"

"I catnap," the Killmaster chuckled. "Marc, I need a car, something with muscle that can be dumped anywhere."

"Can do. Got a Firebird that's disposable."

"Good. Have it in the Kennedy parking lot in an hour. Give me the statistics and the keys in the john across from the Northwest ticket counter."

"An hour," the man replied, and hung up.

Both women waited behind him, bags at their feet.

"Helga, when do you fly again?"

"Tomorrow . . ." She glanced at her watch. "Tonight. London."

"We'll drop you at a hotel near Kennedy. I don't think they'll bother you again, but stay in your hotel until just before your flight. C'mon, we'll get a cab."

He grabbed the bags. Helga turned off lights. At the door, Trilby moved in close.

"Nick, he did take something."

"What?"

"My driver's license and my press card."

At such an early-morning hour, the airport wasn't crowded. As the taxi glided to a stop, the tickle up and down Carter's spine was vibrating a mile a minute. But he still couldn't spot a tail.

Inside the terminal, he eyed a couple of possibles, but dismissed them quickly when they headed for the exits and the taxi stands.

"Good," he muttered under his breath, "They're damn good."

"What do you mean?" Trilby asked, stepping onto the escalator beside him.

"I mean, I know they're here but I can't spot them. I don't mean to brag, but when I know there's a tail on me and I can't spot it, the shadow is the best there is."

They walked the cavernous terminal past two airline ticket areas. As they neared Northwest, Carter transferred the bag to Trilby.

"Buy a pair of tickets for the Seattle flight. Check the bag through, and then meet me down there at the restaurant."

She nodded and they split up. He watched her out of the corner of his eye until she hit the ticket counter. He darted into the rest room.

It was nearly empty. One man was washing his hands, another was patting six or seven hairs over a bald spot, and there was one pair of legs in a stall.

The Killmaster took his time at the urinal, washing his hands, and then combing his hair. Eventually the two loiterers left and he moved to the area in front of the occupied stall.

"Marc?"

"Yeah."

"It's cool."

Carter bent forward as a hand holding an envelope came under the door. He snatched the envelope and stuffed it into his side pocket. Without another word he headed for the door.

Trilby was nearly finished at the counter. Carter went on to the restaurant and ordered a pair of Bloody Marys and a huge breakfast for them both.

Under the table he slit open the envelope and palmed the keys. On the inside of the flap he read: *Black Firebird, two-year-old model, dent right rear fender, lic # LLB-541, Maryland. Section 2, Row B.*

The drinks had arrived and the food was just being served when Trilby slid into her chair.

"Oh, God, I can't eat," she groaned, making a face.

"Eat. It may be a while before we can do it again."

Carter wolfed down the food and finished the home fries she couldn't handle. Over coffee, he laid out the next hour or so.

"We go to the gate, right up to boarding. At the last minute, I kiss you good-bye and take off. You go ahead and get on the plane."

"Get on the plane?" she cried. "What about you?"

He smiled. "Once you're on the plane, my hunch is they'll come after me."

"You meet me in Seattle?"

"No way. Listen. Just before they close the doors and retract the jetway, stick your finger down your throat and empty that breakfast you didn't want anyway into a barf bag. Tell the flight attendant you're sick, too sick to make the flight. The infirmary is on the lower level. They'll take you there."

"Then what?"

"Take about twenty minutes until you're feeling better, and leave. Grab a cab to the Airport Hilton and hide behind a newspaper in the lobby. Pick a chair where you can see the drive in front of the main entrance. I'll pick you up there. It's a black Firebird."

"Are you sure all this will work?"

"Trust me. Let's go!"

The Seattle flight started boarding fifteen minutes after they arrived back in the boarding area. Carter and Trilby got in the middle of the line moving toward the gate. They were five people back when Carter turned and took her in his arms.

She was stiff as a board and her lips were a thin line when he kissed her.

"Have a good flight, honey, see you in a week."

Then he was gone and she was moving down the jetway in a daze.

Carter was alert as he paid the parking fee for the Firebird and drove toward the expressway. Just short of the on-ramp, he veered off onto a side street and gunned the powerful engine.

The car responded and in no time he had reached a wide boulevard where he turned, not back toward Manhattan, but to the right which took him farther out on Long Island. A mile farther on, he cut off onto a smaller street lined with six-story apartment buildings.

Two blocks down, he found a parking spot for the Firebird and darted into the lobby of one of the buildings.

For ten minutes he stood in the lobby and waited. A taxi went by with one passenger in the rear. Then a big Cadillac driven by an elderly woman, and a little Honda driven by a bookkeeper type.

Five minutes more passed and he was about to give up, when the taxi reappeared. It slowed at the Firebird, speeded up, and slowed again across from the doorway where Carter stood.

No wonder he hadn't spotted them. New York is full of cabs. They become part of the background; no one pays any attention to a taxicab.

The driver was big, with blond hair and a strong-featured face. He didn't look like a cabdriver. As the car slowed, he leaned out the window and looked up at the building.

Even at forty yards, Carter could see that his eyes were light blue.

The one in the back was shorter and darker. He looked like a young banker on his way to work.

The two of them seemed to confer, and then they drove a half block on down the street and double-parked. The dark one slid out of the cab and started Carter's way. As he passed the Firebird he did a number through the windows.

When he continued on, Carter filled his hand with his 9mm Luger and moved back under the stairs. He was completely in shadows when the man hit the front door and walked into the lobby. He pulled a pad and pen from his pocket and crossed to the long row of mailboxes.

Carter turned the Luger around and took a firm grip on the barrel, with the butt like a club.

He could hear the man shuffling down the row of mailboxes. He halted just around the corner from where Carter stood. The Killmaster's lungs hurt from not breathing.

His feet moved again and there he stood, right in front of Carter. His eyes went wide when he saw the movement of Carter's arm in the shadows. He uttered a whispered curse and his right hand shot under his coat.

The first blow caught him dead center in the middle of the forehead. Another nailed him in the back of the head on the way down.

He dropped like a stone and Carter went for his pockets. The short-barreled .38 police special he had been going for, Carter slipped into his own pocket. A credentials case told the story: Special Agent J. D. Willis, FBI. The driver's license was the same name, and listed an address in Landover, Maryland.

Carter also pocketed this, and dragged the body under the stairwell.

"Okay, Blondie," he hissed aloud, "let's play *my* game for a while."

Carter left by the front door of the apartment building and ran, straight up, for the Firebird with the keys in his hand. He was in the car by the time Blondie started a U-turn. Carter got the Firebird started and accelerated from the parking space.

The big blond man's eyes went wild when he saw the Firebird hurtling directly at him. Carter could almost read his mind. This wasn't the way it was supposed to be. He was the *hunter*, not the hunted.

At the last second in the game of chicken, the taxi swerved. It went up over a curb, tore up a narrow lawn, and darted through a narrow opening between parked cars back into the street.

Carter did a brodie and came out of it right on the cab's bumper.

"Drive, you bastard," he hissed. "Drive or I'll put you to sleep right here!"

The two cars roared about four blocks before the blond realized that Carter truly meant to nail him. Then he started his maneuvers. Unexpected turns. Sudden stops. A little of everything.

Carter stayed right on his ass, nudging the back bumper of the cab every chance he got.

Then he suddenly pulled a fast U-turn and came back at Carter. Just in time, the Killmaster saw the gun come up. The slug whistled past his neck and tore up a little of the interior upholstery of the Firebird before careening around and finding a home in the rear seat.

Carter shot on past and pulled a U-turn himself. He slammed the Firebird's accelerator to the floor and set the .38 in the well beside him.

They tore down avenues and side streets, wide open all the way . . . twisting, turning, dodging, skidding, burning gas and brakes and rubber as if they were on a speedway. Once he tried to catch Carter again with a U-turn, but Carter wouldn't go for it. Once he slammed on his brakes unexpectedly and jumped out of the cab, and as Carter whizzed past him, he was bent low and pointing his pistol with both hands.

Carter got his head down out of sight and roared past him, but he could hear the explosions and the whine of the shells.

It was a miracle Carter didn't take a hit. When he swung the Firebird back toward Blondie, he had started after Carter on foot, across the street from his cab.

Carter shouted with pleasure as he drove straight at him, anticipating the thrill of smashing him against a building. But Blondie jumped into a doorway as Carter raced down the sidewalk toward him. The Killmaster opted not to go into the doorway after him. When Carter got turned around again, Blondie had made it back to the cab and was off and gathering speed.

Eventually he picked a wide boulevard with nothing in sight, and quit dodging. He just drove straight ahead, almost inviting Carter to tailgate him.

The taxi had about half the oomph of the Firebird. It was no match. Carter bounced him a few times, then pulled over and came up alongside.

About three blocks up was a concrete overpass. Blondie saw it and then turned his head to look at Carter.

He panicked and tried to gain enough speed to get in front.

It was useless.

Carter let him inch up a bit until the taxi was half a length in front. Then he poured the coals to the Firebird, came neck and neck, and sideswiped the taxi.

Blondie tried to brake, but it was too late. He was still hitting about seventy when the cab screamed into the side of the overpass.

It took about fifty feet before Carter could get the Firebird stopped and into reverse. He stopped again right beside the taxi and rolled out.

The cab was accordioned up tight against the concrete, with the transmission housing and some of the engine in the front seat.

Blondie was lying in a lump against the wall where he had been hurtled when the car hit.

Carter approached with the .38 in both hands. Halfway there he knew he wouldn't need a bullet.

The man's head was tucked neatly into his left armpit,

his neckbones broken and parted.

In the distance Carter could hear sirens. He wasted no time. As soon as he had the man's credentials case and wallet, he wiped the .38 clean and dropped it beside the body.

Seconds later, he was back in the Firebird heading toward Kennedy.

Carter didn't even have to honk. Trilby was sitting just inside the door of the hotel. The car was scarcely stopped before she was tugging on the passenger door. She was barely in the seat before Carter was moving.

"What happened?"

He glanced her way. Her face was a pasty white and her teeth were doing a number on her lower lip. Her arms clutched a newspaper to her breasts and her whole body seemed to be vibrating on the seat.

"A lot," he replied, "but you really don't want to know. I'll say one thing, your old man has a lot of people pissed off."

"I know." Her left hand came across and dropped the newspaper across the steering wheel. "Small story, upper-right-hand corner."

It wasn't much, a blurb really, about a once-famous journalist. Her name was Cory Reader, and she had been the victim of a hit-and-run driver.

SIX

"General?"

"Yes, Wynne?"

"Royce didn't check into the Del Rey Beach and Tennis Club. We know he headed south from Los Angeles, but I'm afraid we've lost him."

There was a long pause before the voice on the other end of the line spoke again. "I think we can assume that, with Kirby and D'Ambrosio out of the way and the Reader woman silenced, Josh still has no knowledge of the real plan."

"Yes, sir," Wynne replied. "I think he will still try to stop the assassination."

"Yes, there has been a slight change of plan. The daughter has made contact with another agent, probably a former colleague of Royce's. They eluded our people in New York. We're trying to get a make on the man now, but we have only a description to work with. He isn't with any agency we have a file on, so it's proving difficult. They don't know that *we* know their meeting place, so you should be able to pick them up in Marina del Rey."

"And . . . ?" Wynne asked.

"Eliminate the man. Put Miss Royce under wraps. We have decided to include her in the action. It will add weight to her father's presence."

"I see." Wynne rarely questioned his orders, but this time he felt a qualification was needed. "General, wasn't it Willis and Hornsby on the girl?"

"It was, my boy. Willis is in a coma in a Queens hospital. He has a severe concussion and may not make it."

"And Hornsby?"

"He's dead. Be careful when you take this man, my boy. It would appear that he is quite dangerous."

"I'll do that, General."

Josh Royce had completely changed his appearance. He now looked like an aging hippie as he shambled along the boardwalk in Venice.

To his right, the Pacific lapped lazily at the sand, and bikini-clad girls whirled by him on roller skates.

It had been nearly five years, so he missed the bookshop on his first trip. He spotted the narrow opening on his return.

A sign on the door said OPEN 10:00 A.M. Royce found a café several blocks away and killed a half hour over a cup of coffee.

He returned to the bookshop at a little after ten. The stalls and counters were just as he had remembered them. The dust covers had not been removed from the tables when he pushed through the door.

A little man in slippers emerged from the back through a curtained doorway. He glanced at Royce and adjusted his glasses as he shuffled to the counter.

"Good morning," he said with a gap-toothed smile. "May I help you?"

"Yes. I'm looking for a copy of Milton's *Lost Horizon*. I want the October 1934, Hawthorn Den Prize Edition."

The old man's eyes narrowed and his face filled with surprise. He leaned far forward over the counter, staring intently.

"My God, Josh Royce. It *is* you. I thought they would have buried you by now."

Royce smiled tightly. "They haven't stopped trying, André. I need your help."

"Any time." The old man gripped Royce's hand and shook it vigorously. Then he chuckled. "For a fee, of course."

"Of course. Do you still have the private place?"

"Oh, yes. I am not as active as I used to be, but I still keep the place. Every now and then there are those who need a place to await passage out of the country."

Royce laughed loudly. "You old thief. Which million are you working on now?"

The man shrugged. "The third. I gave up on the first two."

André Girard had been a thief, a fence for stolen goods, and an agent in Paris for ten years when Royce had first met him. When the KGB had gotten too close, it was Royce who was instrumental in moving Girard, his wife, and his daughter to the United States.

In California, the wily old man had merely taken up the same life he had pursued in France. Along the way, Royce had used him several times to cool off Russian defectors coming in from Mexico.

"I will need someone you trust to take the message and bring the people to me."

Girard beamed. "Who else but Louise?"

"Louise?" Royce said. "I thought by now your daughter would have run off to pursue an honest life."

"Oh, she tried, but found it boring. Like me, she had larceny in her soul. Shall we say a thousand dollars a day? That will include everything, of course."

"Done," Royce said.

"Come into the back. We will discuss it over a glass of wine."

Carter wasn't sure when he first awakened because he didn't stay awake long. The room seemed to be filled with the half-light of dawn, so he turned over and went to sleep again. Later, when he opened his eyes for the second time and saw that the light was no better, he lifted his head and realized why.

The blinds were so slanted as to keep out the light from the sky, and now, as he readjusted them, he saw that the sun was high and the morning clear and cloudless.

When he stepped back to glance at his wristwatch on the bedside table and found that it was ten thirty-five, he chuckled softly, not because he found anything humorous in his mistake but simply because he felt so good. It was a purely animal feeling. His mind had not yet begun to work as he arched his back and stretched, coming up on his toes, his fingers reaching for the ceiling and muscles straining pleasurably while he filled his lungs.

It was when he relaxed and blew out his breath that the thoughts started. They came all at once, like a swift-moving panorama, and so therapeutic had been the full night's sleep that he found it hard to accept the remembered sequence of surprise and action and relief that now flooded his mind. Many forgotten details leapt back into focus.

A charter had taken them from Philadelphia to Cleveland. From Cleveland, they had hopscotched to Des Moines, Iowa, where they had holed up in a motel for three hours until they got a direct flight to San Diego. There, Carter had rented a car and they drove up the coast.

He had parked Trilby in a pink stucco monstrosity with phony flamingos by the pool. It was a motel called The Pelican's Roost in Redondo Beach, just close enough to Marina del Rey that they wouldn't look even if they had an inkling.

From there he had driven on into Marina del Rey, where he hit a luggage store, a clothing store, and a drugstore before checking into the Del Rey Beach and Tennis Club just before midnight.

There had been no messages for him, and when he called for Mr. Arnold Pierce, he was told that there was no Mr. Pierce registered.

Two scotches and a quick sandwich later, he was snoring.

Now he was wide awake and a little angry. It was Josh Royce's move, and if the man didn't make it, Carter was all the way across the country with nowhere else to go.

He reached for the phone, got an outside line, and dialed the number he'd memorized the night before from a matchbook.

"Pelican," said a nasal voice.

"Room Nine, please."

There was a shriek of static in his ear and a small voice said, "Hello?"

"It's me. Good morning."

"How is your suite?" Trilby replied dryly.

"Actually, it's very nice. Are you all right?"

"Fine, I guess. The owner's teen-age daughter brought

me some breakfast. I told her I was too sick to leave the room."

"They suspect anything?"

"Only that I'm a hooker on the run from my pimp."

"Good. They won't bother you and you're paid for a week."

"Ugh," she groaned, "I won't be able to stand this place for a week! Any word?"

"No. I'll let myself be seen around the pool and the beach this afternoon. If Josh is anywhere in the neighborhood, he'll find a way to make contact."

"I hope it's soon. The truth is, I'm scared out of my wits."

"Just stay in your room out of sight. Something should pop by tonight."

"Can't I even lay by the pool?"

"No."

"Shit."

"Bye."

Carter rolled out of bed and marched naked into the shower. Five minutes hot, two minutes icy cold, and he was out and unwrapping his drugstore purchases from the night before.

When he had brushed his teeth he went to work with the razor, tipping his head from side to side and frowning at himself as he worked back and forth and up and down, taking one area at a time and searching with his fingertips to make sure that there was no stubble left before moving on. His eyes were busy beneath the frown as he considered the thickness and length of the dark tousled hair. He was overdue for a haircut.

That was good. It was long enough that he could comb it differently. That, and the beginnings of a mustache, would alter his appearance a little.

When he came back into the bedroom, he put a robe on over his nakedness and sat down on the bed. It was now after eleven, and he decided to call room service. Might as well have a little extra breakfast and forget about lunch. He ordered half a grapefruit, toasted English muffins, crisp bacon, three scrambled eggs, and a double order of coffee.

He ate everything, including the marmalade that he hardly ever ate, and dressed.

In the lightweight slacks and a short-sleeved knit shirt, there was no place for the Luger or his sheathed stiletto. Five minutes of searching and he found a place to hide them behind the air-conditioning vent.

Now he was ready to face the day and Josh Royce.

The interior of the Del Rey was as posh and attractive as the Spanish mission-style exterior. Carter wondered as he emerged from the elevator why Royce had chosen this particular haven of the very rich for his meet.

The lobby was practically empty. A quartet of tourists was examining the windows of a souvenir shop at the corner of a short corridor on the right. They were pointing and discussing the merits of something that held their attention that they would probably throw away or toss into the attic and forget when they got home.

The reception desk was small and deserted at the moment, but through an open doorway Carter could see a clerk in shirt sleeves talking with two switchboard operators.

He popped the bell and the man hurried his way, tugging on a blue blazer.

"Yes, sir, can I help you, sir?"

"Yeah. Carter, Suite Six-nineteen. Any messages?"

The clerk checked the cubbyholes and shook his head sadly. "No, sir, nothing."

"If there are, hold them. Don't page me."

"Yes, sir."

Carter moved past a clean and efficient-looking coffee shop, well patronized at the moment, and came to a long carpeted hall on the left that led to an elevator and the ground-floor bedrooms. Still moving and taking stock, he found a formal dining room just ahead, its heavy curtains half closed. Then he was swinging left into a bar and cocktail lounge that resembled dozens of others around the world.

There was a small bandstand with a door beside it, probably leading to dressing rooms, and an even smaller circular dance floor in front of it.

To his right, fifty feet of glass overlooked the expanse of lawn, paved decks, and an enormous swimming pool. Beyond it all was a wide stretch of beach and the ocean.

A small, neat youth in black trousers and a white shirt with a red bow tie appeared at Carter's elbow. "Yes, sir, would you care for a cocktail?"

"Yeah. Beer. Can you put it in a paper cup? I want to walk down to the beach."

"Sure thing."

Carter lit a cigarette and checked the scenery around the pool. It was beginning to fill up for the day. Waiters shuttled drinks from a semicircular snack bar on the terrace to the left. Tall, short, fat, thin—and several perfect—bodies lounged around poolside.

His eye spotted an extremely tall girl, about twenty, in a white hip-length terry coverup approaching from the beach. Besides being beautiful, it was her extremely long legs and her extremely long glossy black hair that drew not only Carter's gaze but the eyes of every other man at the pool.

As she slung the short robe over the back of a chaise, her dark eyes met Carter's through the windows. For a brief second they held, and just before she turned away the Killmaster thought he saw a hint of a smile.

She straightened, the line of breast, shoulders, and chin well defined in profile. She seemed to be looking for something, then made a casual gesture, one arm upstretched.

A pool attendant appeared on the run bearing a long green chair pad and two towels that he spread carefully over the stuffed fabric of the chaise. Carter could see the quick grin from where he stood when she expressed her thanks.

She settled herself with lazy deliberation that spoke of long practice. She ignored the other patrons who were now staring as she opened her oversize beach bag and began to anoint herself with suntan lotion. The white bikini was neither too modest nor too daring, but the sinuous way she caressed her arms and shoulders and thighs was an expert demonstration of latent sex that could hardly be misconstrued.

Once again she glanced Carter's way. This time the smile was in her eyes as well as her lips.

"Your beer, sir."

"Oh, yeah, thanks."

Carter gave him a five and walked out onto the terrace. The girl had gone back to her suntan oil.

Forget it, Carter told himself. *You've got one woman on ice right now, and you can't handle this and a bunch of bad guys turning over rocks everywhere trying to find out who and where you are.*

He walked around the pool and down to the terraced

gardens that led to the beach. He stood at the railing next to the stairs, looking down on the rambling hotel grounds. It was like something William Randolph Hearst might have designed: wide lawns sloping into gardens, and beyond the gardens bungalows facing the oceanfront. Carter surveyed the people and grounds carefully. Nothing.

Behind him, more people clustered around the pool. Waiters scurried drinks from the bar. Two bellboys hurried up the walk from the bungalows, carrying trays and talking. One tray was littered with breakfast dishes, the other with two empty liquor bottles.

It was that kind of a resort.

Carter meandered along the beach for the next hour. No one approached him, no one gave him the eye, and he didn't really see anyone he could tag as the bad guys.

Back at the pool, he was just passing the long, tall brunette in the white bikini when she called loudly to a waiter.

"Yes, ma'am?"

"Yes, I think I'll have something different . . . Jack Daniel's, please, and put a splash of peppermint schnapps in it."

"Jack . . . Daniel's . . . peppermint . . . schnapps?"

"That's right."

"Yes, ma'am."

Carter's neck muscles tensed. He didn't look her way nor did he pause. He just kept moving, right through the lobby onto the elevator and up to his room.

Only one person in the world he had ever met or heard of screwed up good Jack Daniel's sour mash whiskey with peppermint schnapps.

Josh Royce.

SEVEN

Carter swung his feet to the floor, stood, and crossed the room to the tray the waiter had brought. When he had made a weak drink, he downed half of it thirstily and took the glass back to the bed.

It was nearly six o'clock, five hours since he had returned to his room from the pool. In that time he had gone back to the lobby only once, to use a pay phone.

The call went through high-priority lines to Ginger Bateman at the Dupont Circle AXE complex. Her news was informative but not startling.

"It's about the puzzle you intimated when you called me from Des Moines."

"How so?"

"J. D. Willis was considered a bit of a hotshot, but he was also a good agent. Five class-one commendations in the sixteen years he was with the Bureau."

"*Was* with?"

"Yes. He left the Bureau about a year and a half ago to do private research on Communist influence in underdeveloped African countries."

"Contracted by whom?"

"Comrex."

Carter let out a low whistle. "Very interesting. What makes an ex-FBI cop a sudden expert on Reds in Uganda?"

Bateman laughed, but there was no humor in it. "You tell me. I've got some of the best minds around here trying to figure it out. But I've got something even more puzzling."

"Shoot."

"Carl Hornsby. He was a top liaison man for the National Security Agency in Europe. His specialty was Germany, both East and West. His main function was to coordinate intelligence between his own agency and the CIA. And, Nick . . . he was still on the agency's active roster when he bought it."

"Then what the hell was he doing in the States . . . and teamed up with an ex-Bureau agent?"

"He was on special assignment. The odd quirk is, no one seems to know what the special assignment was, or, other than coming from the Pentagon, who ordered it."

"Cute. Absolutely, hilariously cute," Carter growled.

"I've couriered everything up to Hawk in Maine. No word yet, but my guess is he'll want you to run this one to ground. It smells, Nick."

"I plan on it. In the meantime, keep everything in the family. Whatever this Comrex is, they've got big ears."

Carter was replaying the conversation with Ginger Bateman in his mind when the phone went off by his head.

"Yes?"

The voice that answered was feminine and light. "Hi. Just wanted to make sure you were in. I'll be right up."

Carter tried to speak but the immediate click in the receiver told him it was too late. He built himself another drink and waited.

The knock came less than three minutes from the phone call. He opened the door and stood aside. A tall, brassy blonde breezed past him as though the room were hers. He closed the door.

When she whirled to face him he recognized the woman from the pool. Other than her height, the change was pretty radical.

The bikini had been replaced with a figure-hugging black dress that was far from afternoon wear. The bodice was cut low enough so the viewer was able to fully contemplate the shapely fullness of her breasts. The hair—on closer inspection he could see that it was a wig—bordered on platinum, and the makeup had been applied with a heavy hand.

Carter started to speak but she held a finger up to his lips.

"Damn, is this Suite . . . ?" she asked.

Carter went along with it. "Yes."

"But you're not Mr. Cummins."

"I'm afraid not."

She motioned for him to sit. He did. From her purse, she took out a black box about the size of a cigarette pack. From its top she pulled out two antennae extensions and adjusted a single knob. There were two lights on the face of the box. One of them glowed green.

"I suppose he ran out on me," she sighed. "I talked to him last night and he gave me this suite number, said he'd like to take me to dinner tonight. Said it would be a 'most profitable' dinner . . . if you know what I mean."

Carter smiled, lit a cigarette, and relaxed. As she jabbered on, she moved around the room moving the antennae over baseboards, walls, and furniture.

He recognized the device she was using. It was a bug-killer, or field-strength meter. Inside the unit was a highly sensitive radio receiver that could sweep an entire band of frequencies continuously to locate a bug if there was one in the room. The fancy name for it was a spectrum analyzer.

Still verbally working her way around to propositioning Carter, she moved into the bedroom and motioned for him to follow. He had already checked the rooms, but he could have missed a bug if it had been planted by a real pro. The spectrum analyzer would make sure.

Finally, satisfied, she retracted the antennae and turned the instrument off. Then she pointed to the phone.

Carter nodded. "I've already checked both of them."

"Good. I don't think I've made a mistake, but would you have some identification?"

He handed over his true credentials. She examined them and tossed them back. "That's what the man said to look for."

"What man?"

"Josh Royce. Can a girl get a drink around here?"

"Scotch?"

"Super."

They returned to the sitting room. Carter built her one and freshened his own. When he turned back she had her hand extended.

"Louise Girard."

He shook the hand and then filled it with a glass. "Where's Josh?"

"He's a guest of my father's in Venice. We run a little service. Josh hired us this morning. If Josh wants you to know more, he can tell you himself."

She sipped her drink with finality. Suddenly, Carter liked her as well as admired her. She was no-nonsense and she knew what she was doing.

"When?" he asked.

"Tonight. At nine o'clock you go down to dinner. At ten the entertainment starts. It's a female singer and a trio from Mexico City. They don't make a lot here, so the singer is open to side money. I've already made the arrangements."

"Can you trust her?"

"No reason not to. I'm married, you're my lover. We have to meet secretly."

Carter sipped his drink. "Lovely."

"You fall madly in love with her during the ten o'clock show. So much so that you buy her a drink. After the midnight show, she takes you back to her bungalow. The garden patio behind the bungalow has a door in the wall. There's a small alley on the other side of the wall. I'll be there in a car."

Carter smiled. "Are all the bungalows that way?"

"Yes."

"I can see why Josh chose this place."

She nodded. "Earlier I cased everybody casing you at the pool."

"And . . . ?"

"A couple. He's tall, good shoulders, about forty, with a movie-star face and salt-and-pepper hair. She's short, a little plump, with red hair."

Carter nodded. "I saw them. That's about all."

"That's just it. They were trying to make somebody, but they didn't. They checked you out, but they also checked every man in the place who even came close to you in appearance."

"Good," he said. "That means they have a description but not a sure make."

She headed for the door. "I take it you've got Josh's daughter stashed somewhere else?"

He nodded. "Redondo Beach, a motel."

She opened the door and spoke in a loud voice. "You're a real generous gentleman, lover. Call me any afternoon!"

She took off down the hall with a hip-swinging walk that nearly bounced off the walls on both sides of the hall.

The *maître d'* was bored. A twenty got Carter a smile, a bow, and a front table near the dance floor and bandstand.

The dinner was edible and that was about all, but he managed to make it—and an overpriced bottle of wine—last nearly the whole hour between nine and ten.

Over coffee and a good brandy, the trio came out and played a medley of Spanish and Mexican folk songs that led into Consuelo Cortez.

Her lobby picture didn't do her justice. She was tall, with wavy black hair down to her shoulders and the kind of ripe, sultry figure that is so often found in Latin women who haven't let themselves go to fat.

In short, she was breathtaking.

She sang with the combo, first a hot jazz number in Spanish, then a bluesy medley in English. She had a fine voice and Carter almost forgot what he was really there to do.

She sang for nearly an hour. When she started to leave the stage, the applause brought her back for a well-deserved encore.

As she started a medley from *Carmen*, Carter beckoned his waiter.

"The singer is terrific."

"Yes, sir," the waiter replied with a slight upward roll to his eyes.

"I wonder if she would join me for a drink when she has finished her set."

The man shrugged. "I doubt it, sir. Señorita Cortez is a little uptight about mingling with the customers. But I could ask."

He had his tongue so far in his cheek Carter thought he had mumps. The Killmaster pumped his hand like a hot-blooded Shriner and left a fifty in his palm.

"You see what you can do."

"I'll do my best, sir."

Consuelo sang two more songs, then left the stage. Carter saw the waiter stop her and gesture in his direction. A moment later she was walking straight for his table. Carter got to his feet and waited for her to approach.

"Thank you for coming," he said in Spanish. "Won't you permit me to buy you a drink? I am called Nick."

"Thank you," she said in English.

The waiter, who had followed her, held the chair and she sat down.

"I am Consuelo Cortez. You are a salesman, no?"

"Yes."

She nodded at the waiter and he left. "Do you mind if we speak English?" she asked. She had a charming accent. "I would like to speak it better than I do."

"Not at all," Carter said. "My Spanish isn't too good. I enjoyed your singing very much. I hope you don't mind that I asked you to join me for a drink?"

She laughed. "Not at all. You might even be an American movie producer."

"For once in my life I'm sorry I'm not," he said, smiling.

She shrugged. "Well, you are still an attractive man and I am here."

The waiter came and put a glass of wine in front of her. Carter motioned for him to bring another drink and he left.

"I do two shows," Consuelo said. "Until the last one is over I do not drink anything but wine. You liked my singing, no?"

"Yes."

"Someday I will be a big star. That is why I wish to speak English better."

"I'm sure you will be," Carter said. "When do you do your next show?"

"In one hour. Then I sing no more. After the midnight set people are drinking too much to enjoy good singing, and they have two other singers. Not good voices but what you call hot."

The waiter brought his drink. Carter lifted it and looked at her. "To a lovely woman with a lovely voice," he toasted.

"Thank you, senõr," Consuelo said.

They drank, and when she put her glass down it was empty.

"Another one?" Carter suggested.

She shook her head. "I must go and rest before my next show. I am sorry."

"Perhaps you'll join me again after your next set?"

She smiled. "Perhaps."

Carter stood up as she left. He noticed the envious look from several single men at nearby tables.

For a while the combo switched to dance music. It was just a little after midnight when they switched back to Latin jazz and Consuelo appeared again.

She did a forty-minute set right to Carter, as if he were the only customer in the room. Again he was impressed with her voice and her presence. Under different circumstances he would have liked a different ending to the evening.

When she left the stage she came directly to Carter's table. He stood as she was seated. He was scarcely back in his chair when a glass of wine arrived for her.

He leaned forward and whispered in a low voice. "Is everything set?"

"Of course."

"You really are very beautiful and very talented. If I'm ever in Mexico City . . ."

She leaned forward, the smile still sweet on her angelic face. "Forget it. I've never been in Mexico City and I don't ever expect to be. My real name is Maria O'Brien. I'm thirty five years old and I've got a lazy, drunken Irishman for a husband and three kids. If I didn't have this gig I'd be flat-backing it in San Diego to put food on the table."

Carter sighed, leaned back, and spoke in a normal voice. "Would you like another glass of wine?"

"I don't know," she said, looking around. "Do you like it here?"

"I have since you sat down. Why?"

"I don't like to stay in a club after I have finished working. I would rather be in a quiet place where we could just talk."

"Talk?" he said.

She shrugged. "I'll get my wrap and meet you by the pool."

She was gone.

Carter paid the bill. As he walked to the rear door that led to the terrace and the pool, he checked the other males. Most of them had their chins on their chests.

He spotted the tall, muscular man with the salt-and-pepper hair and his plump redheaded wife at a corner table. They must have come in during the second show.

The man seemed to be studying Carter, weighing him, as he passed the table. The redhead was checking out the rest of the room.

A couple of minutes later Consuelo joined him, a light jacket around her shoulders. They were silent past the pool and down through the gardens. Beside him, her perfume seemed to fill the air around his head.

At the bungalow, she fumbled in her purse for keys.

"I really meant it, you know."

"What?"

"You are very talented."

Consuelo rolled her head to the side and upward until her eyes met his. She was wearing a smile, a real one. "Thanks."

Inside the bungalow she headed directly for the bedroom. "The bar is there. Fix yourself something and me a gin."

"Gin and what?" Carter asked.

"Gin and gin."

She disappeared. He fixed the drinks and followed her.

She was standing beside the bed. Just as he hit the door, the red sheath she had been wearing slithered down over her hips to puddle at her feet. The bra and panties she wore beneath it were barely there, emphasizing rather than concealing her gorgeous body tanned to a perfect bronze.

The light was on. Carter noticed the drapes over the windows above the bed were gaped open a full two feet.

"Your drink."

She turned and took it. "There are two keys there on the night table. One is to the patio doors; the other is to the door in the rear wall."

"I understand."

"Good. Get undressed," she said, and tipped the glass.

Her breasts were big and heavy in the lace cups that tried to hold them in. When she moved they bobbled halfway out of the thin fabric containing them. Her belly was slightly mounded and set with a deep navel.

"You know something, lady? You sure as hell don't look like you've had three kids."

She set the glass down, laughed, and patted her belly. "Hell, number four's on the way. Kiss me!"

He did, and during it she managed to remove both his underwear and her own.

"Now get in bed."

He did, and watched the show as she made the long cross to the light switch. Seconds later she was in the bed, turning her back to him and fluffing the pillow.

"See you in the morning."

Carter got the picture. He slid from the bed, dressed, and grabbed the keys.

He was on his knees by the bed. A small streak of moonlight came through the window, leaving a silver lance across the slope of her body beneath the covers.

He couldn't resist. He brushed his lips across hers. "Good night, little mother."

She chuckled. "Love your woman well."

He locked the patio door behind him and moved to the wall. The wooden door unlocked and opened soundlessly.

Directly across the alley was a compact station wagon, its lights off, its engine idling. He saw Louise Girard motion to him and he nodded in reply.

Quickly, he locked the garden door and, in a crouch, ran for the wagon. She had the door open and he dived in, pulling it shut behind him.

"Get down on the floor."

With Carter's bulk it wasn't easy, but he managed and the car took off. He hunched his knees up, put his arms around them, and bowed his head.

They moved along for what seemed to be about a block and a half or two blocks, and then stopped. After a few seconds they turned left. After another left they moved more steadily for a matter of a few miles, and then there was a longer wait. This, plus the awareness that more light was filtering into the car, told Carter that they might be turning onto the freeway. When he heard the sound of trucks he was sure of it.

He couldn't tell how long they stayed on the freeway, but again there came a left turn followed by a repetition of starts and stops similar to the first part of the journey.

When he became tired of counting turns, he became impatient for the trip to be over.

"How much longer? I think I've shrunk five inches."

"Just a few minutes."

The car slowed and made what seemed like a sharp and cautious turn. The sound of the engine took on a different character, as though the street had suddenly narrowed. A little farther on they stopped and she left her seat. Somewhere at one side there was the sound of a door sliding back, and when Louise returned she put the car into reverse. Seconds later they stopped and again there was the sound of the door. Finally she stepped out and tapped Carter on the shoulder.

"All right, we're there."

He scrambled out and arched the kinks out of his back, aware now that he was in a small garage. He let himself be led around the front of the car. Behind him the light in the garage was snapped off and he could hear the lock click as the door swung behind him.

He counted thirty-eight paces before the passageway jogged left for a few feet and then turned right again to end at a heavy-looking wooden door. A push button was recessed in the frame on the right and he watched Louise push it three times, hesitate, then add a final long ring.

A lock clicked and Carter found himself face to face with an old man in a well-worn brown tweed suit.

"Nick Carter, my father, André Girard," Louise said, and disappeared down the hall.

"Welcome to our modern underground railway, Mr. Carter. Follow me, please."

The old man turned and mounted a long flight of steps to another door. Carter followed him through the second door, into a kitchen. It was a squarish room that had another door at the rear, apparently leading to a porch of some kind. As Carter hesitated, Girard stepped past him and gestured toward a pair of swinging doors in the wall on the left.

"This way, please."

Carter followed him into a dining room and turned right into a hall. Directly ahead a staircase led down to what apparently was the street entrance. A second staircase led to the floor above. On the left was a small room that might have been a study. There seemed to be crates everywhere.

"Nice place for a hideout," Carter quipped.

The old man chuckled. "For a thousand a day I like to make my guests comfortable. Right through that door there."

He shuffled off down the hall in his floppy slippers, and Carter entered the room.

It was a comfortably furnished room that looked lived

in. Two good-sized, priceless Oriental rugs nearly covered the floor from wall to wall. The chairs were antique, the divan that stood at the front between two tall windows was Queen Anne and would probably fetch ten thousand at an auction. Authentic old masters adorned the walls, and the books were leather-bound right out of an old English manor house.

"Nick, am I glad to see you!" Josh Royce came from behind a leather bar, a glass in his hand. "Chivas is your drink, isn't it?"

"Yeah," Carter said, "it is."

He took the drink with his left hand and buried his right, clear to the wrist, in Josh Royce's gut.

EIGHT

Royce gasped for about five minutes and finally struggled to his feet. He staggered to one of the elegant high-backed chairs and dropped into it with a wheezing groan.

"Now, why the hell did you do that?"

"General principles, you old bastard. There are bodies all over the landscape, your daughter is scared shitless, and I had to kill an American NSA agent to save my own skin. On top of all that, I'm not supposed to lift a finger inside the continental United States and you know it. Now, suppose you tell me just what the hell is going on."

"Just what I need, a smartass," Royce replied, moving to the bar and holding his belly. "Where's Trilby?"

"A fleabag called The Pelican's Roost in Redondo Beach, and she's as pissed off at you as I am."

Royce made one of his horrible Jack Daniel's and schnapps drinks and saluted Carter with the glass. "I may be a fuck-up so far, but you came."

"Yeah, I came, and I can leave just as fast."

"All right, Nick, all right. Believe me, I didn't think

it was going to turn out like this myself. How much do you know about Comrex?"

"What we have in our files and what I got from Trilby's research."

"That's a big chunk of it, but without the key people and the key objectives."

"Which are?" Carter said, sliding onto one of the bar stools.

"Comrex has key people ready to take power in practically every central and southern African nation except South Africa itself. When the first country topples, it will be a base of operations and the others will go down like dominoes. The key is the first country. It's targeted, and the ball starts rolling in four days."

"Where?"

"In Mexico, Puerto Vallarta."

Carter set his drink down and rubbed his temples. "Comrex is going to start an operation to take over most of Africa in Puerto Vallarta, Mexico?"

Royce took the stool beside Carter and spread a map out on the bar. "It's only half as crazy as it sounds."

Carter leaned over the map. It was Africa. Several of the countries from Botswana in the south on up to the Congo had been outlined in different colored inks. A heavy black line had been drawn from Dar es Salaam in Tanzania in the east, to Cabinda on the west coast of the Republic of the Congo. The island nation of Madagascar, or the Malagasy Republic, in the Indian Ocean off Africa's eastern coast, had been outlined in heavy red ink.

"A lot of what I'm about to tell you is supposition, Nick, but a lot of it is fact. Understand one thing. I think the base of operations they want is here, in Madagascar. It's an island; it can be defended easily. And Mozambique, Rhodesia, Zambia, and Tanzania are only hours away."

"I'm listening," Carter said, "but what I'm hearing is crazy."

"Not so much as you'd think. It's ripe. With its economy shaky, malnutrition among its children rampant, its life-giving rain forests almost totally depleted, and its existence dependent upon clove and vanilla exports, Madagascar has looming before it the spectre of being another Ethiopia."

Royce gulped the remainder of his drink, rubbed his thumbs into his eyes, and continued.

"The current government is shaky to say the least. They readily accept aid and anything else they can get from both the East and the West. Recently, it had been rumored that, in return for more aid, the Soviets have requested—and obtained—permission to construct several secret submarine bases on the island's western coast."

Carter help up a hand. "Wait a minute. That rumor has been there for years. It's never been substantiated."

"Right," Royce replied. "But lately it's been fanned out of all proportion. There's a reason for that, Nick. With refueling bases in that area, the Soviets could triple their power in the Indian Ocean. That shakes a lot of people up in Washington, and it's meant to. Because of it, a lot of people would like to exercise more clout in Madagascar. That's where Comrex has stepped in."

Carter lit a cigarette from the one he had going. "On the surface, that makes Comrex the good guys, Josh."

The older man grinned and moved behind the bar to rebuild both their drinks. "But we know different, Nick. If nothing else, because of the methods they've already used. It's just those methods that made me start to ask questions and eventually split."

"Just how did you get involved with Comrex?"

"I'll explain that in a minute. Right now I'm going to give you a history lesson. The ethnic background of Madagascar comes from migrating coastal African tribes and peoples of Indonesia. There have always been a lot of internal wars. In 1960, the country obtained its independence from France. Since then, it has been a republic with a socialist government."

Carter nodded. "So what? It's probably the only form of government they can live with."

"True," Royce replied, "but socialist is only a step away from communist, and that makes the far right pee in their pants. Believe me, I know; I was there."

"And you're not now."

Royce shrugged. "Call it old age."

"Okay, I'll bite," Carter replied. "What's the scenario for Comrex to take control?"

"Bevello Aldami."

Carter's face stayed blank. "I'll bite again. Who the hell is Bevello Aldami?"

"He is the wealthy playboy scion of the most powerful family on the island. He's also the last living descendent of the ancient ruling Hova clan that ruled Madagascar as royalty hundreds of years ago. When the elder Aldami died, it was only natural that Bevello would take up the family's mantle. Nick, there is a strong faction that would like to see Bevello Aldami crowned king."

"What? *King?*"

"That's right, kind of a benevolent dictator. A lot of people—in and out of the country—think that's the only solution. There has long been a tight-lipped truce between the government's ruling political power and the Aldami family."

Carter shook his head. "Third World politics . . . not my strongest suit. Where does Bevello stand?"

"He's known to be anti-socialist, anti-communist, and pro-West. Right now, Washington is neutral on the question, but people in the know would like to keep things just the way they are—don't rattle the cage, so to speak."

"But Comrex wants it different."

"Right. And, Nick, they plan on using Bevello Aldami to change things and gain power for themselves."

"Now we get to the nitty-gritty."

"Exactly," Royce sighed. "Nick, when I say Aldami is wealthy, I mean the guy is *loaded*. He's truly jet set. When he's not popping to all the watering holes around the world in his personal 707, he's on his yacht. It's a converted minesweeper called the *Hova Palace*. He's got a hobby that he's passionate about, and that's how Comrex is going to nail him."

"In Puerto Vallarta?"

"Right. He's crazy about Incan, Aztec, and Mayan art. The *Hova Palace* is in Acapulco right now. Day after tomorrow, it sails for Puerto Vallarta. Sometime after it arrives, Aldami is planning on visiting a gallery there. A special showing is planned, exclusively for him, of Mayan artifacts. Nick, that's where they're going to hit him—in that gallery."

"Hit him . . . ?"

Royce nodded. "Comrex is going to assassinate Aldami and somehow make it look like the Soviets did the job."

Carter was beginning to put it together. "That would fan the sub base rumor even more. The politicos in

Washington would want action. We go in as a protectionist force."

"You got it," Royce said. "Comrex is in position. They would get the job—covertly, of course. But once they're in, possession is nine tenths and so forth. They answer to Washington on the surface, but while they do that they're planning on taking over the rest of Africa."

"How do they plan on pinning the assassination of Aldami on the Russians?"

Royce's face lost a little color. "That's what Jack Kirby and Vince D'Ambrosio tried to find out for me."

"And Kirby's dead."

Royce nodded. "So is D'Ambrosio. I saw his body two nights ago in L.A."

"And Cory Reader?"

"Same thing," Royce replied tightly. "Cory had all the facts. She was putting the chain of command together, right to the top. My guess is she did it, but they got to her before she could get what she found to me."

Carter took his drink and paced the room. What Royce was saying was wild and farfetched, but Carter had seen similar schemes before. Such a plan was feasible even if it sounded crazy.

"How did you get involved, Josh?"

"I was still with the Company. If you remember a few years ago, all the mess? Our hands were tied, congressional investigations, budget cuts, none of us could move anymore. I got sick of it and I was pretty vocal about it. I got a sudden assignment in Lisbon. It turned out that the assignment was shit. But I was contacted by Comrex."

"Who?"

"Carmen San Filippo."

This got Carter's attention. Carmen San Filippo was

the daughter of one of the most powerful men in the old Franco regime. If anything, she was more of a staunch Fascist than her father had been. The Basques had assassinated the elder San Filippo years before. Since that time, and with the onset of a more liberal government in Spain under King Juan Carlos, Carmen had emigrated to Lisbon. There she had used her contacts and her wealth to bring down any government in the world that even hinted at leaning toward communism or socialism. Her methods had brought her to the attention of AXE several times.

"Carmen San Filippo is a Fascist fanatic, Josh."

Carter's comment brought a shrug and a weary nod from the other man. "I know. But at the time, I was disgusted and pissed off. She told me that if I had any pet projects, she could help get them done and avoid Company rules."

"And she did?"

"In spades," Royce replied. "I guess I got sucked in. When my retirement came up, Comrex offered me a job with more money and more ways to get things done than I ever dreamed possible."

"Then it went sour?"

Royce nodded. "Yeah, it went sour when I realized Comrex's excesses were exactly what Congress and the American people were hot about. A lot of people died, Nick, because of some of the things I did. It turned out a lot of those people were doing a hell of a lot more good than they were harm."

"You took your orders from San Filippo?"

"Only until I got into the inner circle. I learned then that her primary function was recruitment. But my orders always came from Lisbon."

Carter mulled this over. "That might help, eventually.

Cory Reader didn't get her findings to you, Josh, but do you have any idea about the top chain of command?"

"I know it's heavy into the Pentagon and NSA. I know they have agents, top agents, in almost every agency on their side. I had a lot of orders from a guy called Cornwall, Jeffrey Cornwall. He was a bird colonel then."

"And now?"

"He's head of NATO Command for the bases we still have in Portugal."

"Jesus," Carter hissed.

"Let me tell you something else, Nick, an example of how infiltrated they are. Comrex has the military and law enforcement codes for computers all over the world. They can copy telexes at will. They can also put out a fugitive warrant on anybody, anywhere. And, Nick, you can't hide from them. For instance, use your credit card in Paris or Tijuana . . . in minutes they've got you pinpointed."

"So that's why you need me?"

"Right," Royce replied. "I did a little checking on you after I worked with you a few years ago. It was interesting. I didn't find you anywhere. Officially, you don't exist, and whatever agency you work for doesn't exist. If I couldn't nail you, then I don't think Comrex can. If we're going to stop them, Nick, we need contacts and funds. I think you can get those contacts and funds. Am I right?"

Carter thought about this for a few seconds, and then moved in close to Royce, until his face was only inches from the other man's.

"How do I know you're not conning me, Josh? How do I know you're not still working for Comrex and suckering me in?"

Eyeball to eyeball, he stared back at Carter, a wry grin

turning his lips downward at the corners. "I guess you don't. But I'll offer you two reasons you should. No matter what you think of me, Nick, I wouldn't put this kind of heat on Trilby unless I thought it was damn important."

"And the second reason?"

"Three, really. Jack Kirby, Vince D'Ambrosio, and Cory Reader. Jack and Vince I trained; they were like sons. Cory was a lush, but I was probably the only real friend she ever had. I don't fuck my friends, Nick."

Carter didn't blink for several seconds, and neither did Josh Royce.

What the other man said made sense. The Killmaster decided the best option was to believe him.

"Okay, pal, let's figure out a way to save this playboy's ass."

"General, there has not been a woman even remotely resembling Trilby Royce anywhere near the Del Rey Beach and Tennis Club."

"And the agent?"

"If he has arrived, he has done nothing to contact Royce, nor has Royce tried to contact him. I've paid off three informers on the staff and we have three people on surveillance. Every man remotely resembling the agent's description has been watched. Nothing."

"I don't see how any contact could have been made. The Royce girl and the agent have been on the run. So has Josh. We're monitoring everything from this end, and we've gotten nothing."

"And, General, I think we have another problem. We've completely lost Royce. It's as if he's disappeared."

The silence was deadly from the other end of the line.

Wynne felt sweat run down his back. He knew that when the reply came it would be an explosion.

To his surprise, it was just the opposite. "I wouldn't worry too much about that, Wynne. We have a profile on Royce a mile long. Psychologically, I think we can predict his every move even if we can't witness it."

"Then you think he'll still move south?"

"I do. How many people have you working?"

"Eighteen of our own."

"Keep them on it. You and Cruz head on down to Mexico. The woman is in place. Make contact and give her the green light. Josh obviously has help now that we can't identify. We'll just make that work somehow in our favor."

"Yes, sir."

As usual, the phone went dead in Wynne's ear. He hung up and turned to Cruz and the couple. Quickly he explained the gist of the telephone conversation.

The tall, handsome man with the salt-and-pepper hair merely nodded. The plump redhead stood and spoke with a certain degree of defiance in her voice.

"Ya know, just once, I would like to know who the hell it is I'm working for!"

"Loretta," Wynne said in a quiet, calm voice, "do you or don't you have a cushy government job making four times the money you would normally make?"

"Yes, but—"

"And tell me, Loretta, are you or are you not far too stupid to have ever gotten that job if Comrex hadn't interceded for you in the first place?"

"Goddammit, I resent—"

Wynne's arm swung. The flat of his palm hit her cheek like a rifle shot. Her body made three complete revolutions before it crashed into the opposite wall and slid to the floor.

"Raymond . . . ?"

"Yes, sir," the tall man said, jumping to his feet.

"When your pig of a wife wakes up, remind her again that she is not indispensable."

"Yes, sir, I'll do that, sir."

Wynne and Cruz walked from the room. Raymond stepped over his plump wife's inert body and poured himself a drink. He had to hold it with both hands to get the glass to his lips.

NINE

It was nearly nine when Carter awoke in the morning. It was several seconds before he remembered that he was not alone. Consuelo was still asleep, her dark face beautiful in repose. She hadn't even stirred when he had slipped back into the bedroom and the bed just before dawn.

He slipped out of bed and went to take a shower. When he returned she was awake, stretching like a cat and kicking the covers off. She was wearing a pair of dark blue pajamas she must have put on after he had left.

"What would you like for breakfast?" Carter asked.

"Whatever you have," she replied, moving past him with a smile.

He called room service and ordered a melon, scrambled eggs, toast and coffee for two. She joined him in a robe just as the waiter was leaving.

"He has big feet."

"What?"

"Your lover's husband," she replied. "He has big feet. I heard him leave from under my window."

"Oh," Carter grunted, and stuffed food in his mouth.

She didn't speak again until they were finishing the

coffee. "She will leave her husband for you someday, your girlfriend?"

"I don't think so. Kids, security, you know."

Consuelo sighed. "Oh, God, do I know."

He decided the time was right. "How much longer is your gig here?"

"Tonight is the last night."

"Good. How would you like to make another two hundred tonight?"

"Suits me."

"And do you have any friends in the area?"

"I have a sister in Santa Monica."

"How would she like to make some easy money?"

"How?"

"Same way. Does she live alone?"

"Yes."

"Good," Carter replied. "Call her, and here's what I want you to tell her . . ."

Consuelo returned ten minutes later from the phone. "She says either you're nuts or you're awfully horny."

"A little of both," Carter chuckled, leaning over the table and kissing her on the nose. "What's your sister's name?"

"Nadine. She'll be cruising the Black Bucket about one o'clock."

In the lobby, Carter made straight for the head bellman with a palmed fifty. "I want a car and driver for the day. Can that be arranged?"

"Sure."

"Make sure the driver knows where the afternoon action is."

"What kind of action you want?"

Carter winked. "Need you ask?"

"Got ya, buddy. He'll be out front in an hour."

In a phone booth, Carter called the AXE hot line on

Dupont Circle and got Bateman on the first ring.

"They haven't tagged me yet, but after tonight they will," he said.

"That's not because they haven't been trying," Bateman replied. "Your description is flying around every corner in town. They'll make you soon, Nick, even without tapping our computers."

"Hopefully it will be too late by then. Recorder on?"

"Of course."

For the next ten minutes, Carter talked rapid-fire. He related everything from Josh Royce, the man's suspicions, and his own evaluation.

"You still there, Ginger?"

"Yeah, I'm here. Some yarn."

"I'm afraid it's more than a yarn. Jump on that inquiry about my ID, and try and find out where it's coming from."

"Already have. Anything else?"

"Yeah. Cash."

"How much?"

"Twenty thou, in hundreds and fives."

"Jeez, Nick, are you going to knock them off or buy them off?"

He ignored her. "It has to be cash, no trace."

"Okay. What else?"

"A man and his boat, probably for a week. That's it."

"Call you back in ten minutes."

It was five.

"Cigar stand in the Tierney Building on Wilshire Boulevard. You're the man who ordered the twenty back issues of *Playboy*. It's called Kurt's News. See Kurt."

"Got it," Carter said. "What about the boat?"

"It's a new marina just south of downtown Long Beach, called the Tradewinds. The boat is *California Dreamin'*, and the owner is Rocco Parks. You're expected, but he knows nothing."

"You're a doll."

"I know. Try to remember how you spend the twenty grand."

"Hell," Carter said laughing, "I'll get receipts."

He hung up and hit his room. After a quick shave he changed from nighttime clothes into daytime clothes and returned to the lobby. The head bellman nailed him at the elevator.

"It's a new brown Cougar right outside. Driver's name is Mitch. He's my brother-in-law, and, man, whatever you want he'll find it for ya!"

"You're a champ," Carter said, and headed for the door.

The bellman waited until he saw the Cougar pull out, and then picked up the house phone.

"Hello."

"Yes, sir," the bellman replied. "Carter just took off with my brother-in-law. I clued him in. When they get back I'll have a record of every place he went and everyone he talked to."

"Good, good. And the other two?"

"Out bagging rays by the pool and trying to score, same as yesterday."

"You're doing a good job. Tell your brother-in-law I'll take care of him."

"Thanks."

The bellman hung up and shook his head. *Private eyes,* he thought, *they're all wacko, looking for a guy and they don't even know who he is. Well, what the hell, if they wanna give me a bill a day to keep track of three yahoos on vacation, who am I to argue?*

Mitch turned out to be a good driver but a lousy snoop. Carter would hit a joint and Mitch would still have his little notebook out making a notation of the name when the Killmaster returned to the car. His excuses not to hit the inside while Carter was having a drink and smooching the girls were also amateurish.

It was about what he had expected. Comrex, no matter how big, wouldn't have the manpower to cover every guy at the hotel close to Carter's description. They had to recruit locally, and Mitch was the best they could do on short notice.

After the sixth joint along the Sunset Strip, Carter oozed into the back seat of the Cougar and leaned over the front.

"Mitch, my man, the bartender in there says the kind of exotic pulchritude I am searching for can be found along Washington Boulevard near Culver City."

"Christ, bud, if ya just want a piece of cooze, I know every cathouse on the east side."

"Mitch, my man, do not be crude. Cooze I do not desire. Pulchritude with certain raw class is my current need. What about Washington Boulevard?"

Mitch turned away from Carter's breath and wheezed, "Yeah, there's a four-block strip down there they call 'boy's town.' I call it the 'combat zone.' But you're the boss."

"Then drive on, my man, drive on!"

It took about twenty minutes to drop down from Sunset to Washington. In the back seat, Carter hummed—off-key—all the way and acted more sloshed by the block.

He hit two more places before he spotted a sign for the Black Bucket. "Mitch, my friend, that looks a likely place."

"It's the pits among the pits . . ."

"Good show! Pull in!"

The inside was black-inside-a-mine dark. In the foyer, Carter peeled off a fifty to pay a five-dollar cover. It went to a teen-ager behind a cage with six pounds of silicone leering through a wide-net top. He tipped her a second five, then went to the bar and ordered a beer.

"Glass?"

"Christ, no."

Two stools away, a middle-aged man with gray hair and good clothes was leaning toward a busty redhead on the stool next to him. Beyond, three young men were going it stag and drinking beer. Two Air Force sergeants occupied the next stools, and then there was a gap until the bar curved at the front.

Planted on the corner stools were three overdressed women who were half turned from the bar so that they could look through the open street door and, if it seemed advisable, offer their smiles and inviting nods to any passing male who looked susceptible and seemed in need of encouragement.

The beer came and Carter paid with a twenty.

While doing his sidework, the bartender paid Carter a lot of attention. The girl with the fabulous chest must have clued him in that Carter had paid with a fifty off the top of a thick wad.

About ten minutes passed, and he commented offhandedly, "Looking for some afternoon fun?"

"Maybe," Carter replied, grinning.

"All free-lancers," the bartender said, waving his hand down the bar and across the tables where the "ladies" sat smiling and adjusting their cleavage.

"I'm very particular," Carter replied.

The bartender shrugged and moved away. Carter checked the room some more.

It was a motley crew. Besides the table occupants, there were six girls moving with boredom and elevated heels around the room. Besides having boredom as a common trait, they all had massive bosoms.

Some doctor in west L.A. was getting massively rich off his plastic pump gun.

Carter didn't spot anyone who matched Consuelo's description of her sister.

In the course of another beer, two girls dropped by with straight-out propositions: fifty bucks for a one-shot, a hundred for the rest of the afternoon.

Carter declined. "I'm looking for the girl of my dreams."

A guy in black leather with chains for a belt and long, stringy hair moved down from the end of the bar. He stood in front of Carter and rubbed his crotch.

"Hi."

"Good-bye," Carter said.

He was followed by a possible: short, full figure, short skirt, with a cute face and oodles of long black hair.

"Mind if I sit down?"

Carter shrugged.

"What's your name?"

"Nick."

Her eyes seemed to light up. "Nice name. I only do this now and then. I'm a junior at UCLA."

Carter smiled. "Good for you."

"Ever try a three-way, honey?" She pointed out her boyfriend at a nearby table. "He's a football player. We really have a ball, and it's not so high, either, with him along, you know? Sharing's not like you bought something all for your own use."

"You and your boyfriend?"

"Yeah, sure, that's what I'm talking about. Three of us, and we switch around all kinds of ways. How about it, huh? The three of us, and if you've got a place we can go, sixty bucks for the rest of the afternoon."

Carter gave her his meanest grin. "Where do you roll me, honey? On the way, and take my car to sell in

Mexico? . . . or just my cash and credit cards after we get to the room?"

She hardly blinked. She moved back a step, cocking her head, then nodded. "I knew I was right. I've been watching you, big man. You're a goddamn closet case. Girls aren't your bag. You dig boys."

"Get lost, honey."

She shrugged and her massive bosom swayed heavily. "Then I guess you can go hang around the toilet till one of your own kind picks you up." She shook her head. "Goddamn fags. You bastards are ruining us working girls!" She turned away and Carter faced the bar to finish his drink. It was gone, replaced by a full one, and more of his money was gone.

He had almost decided that little Nadine had let him down, when he spotted what had to be her coming out of the rest room. She was about five-four and a little overweight, with all of it packed into a sweater and skirt at least one size too small. Under too much makeup she had a dark, pixieish face and nice eyes.

Their eyes locked and Carter smiled. She returned it and headed his way. He faced the back bar and concentrated on his drink. Still not looking at her face, he saw her open a bag and take out a pack of cigarettes. When she had selected one, she tapped it, put it between her fingers, and waited. So did Carter, because he knew what would happen next. It took only five seconds.

"Could I have a light, please?"

He gave her a light and she said thank you, and took a sip of water. For the moment she didn't seem to be particularly aware of him.

"Is that water?"

"Yes."

"Wouldn't you rather have a drink?"

"I only drink champagne . . . with my friends."

Carter rolled on the stool to face her. "Then let's be friends. I'm Nick."

"I'm Nadine."

"Bartender . . . champagne."

It came fast, and Carter guessed the tab would be at least forty bucks.

"To friendship," she said, raising the glass.

"To getting to know each other better," Carter said, and, now that she was closer, checked her out completely.

He saw now that the glossy hair had a sleek and pinned-back look, that she had a rather pretty face in spite of the heavy makeup and the slackness around the mouth and under the chin.

Because the light was bad he couldn't be sure how old she was, but it seemed to him she wasn't much more than twenty. The snugness of the clothes accentuated the noticeable bosom and hips, but she was well proportioned and not yet fat. Three bracelets loaded with assorted charms were stacked on her right wrist and clinked and jingled when she moved her arm. On the third finger on the left hand was a gold ring with a topaz as big as a domino.

When he brought his glance up, the painted mouth was smiling at him but the eyes remained speculative.

"Satisfied?" she asked.

"Almost. Nice ring."

"My sister gave it to me."

He leaned forward. He brushed his lips across her ear. "How far is your apartment?"

"Twenty minutes, Santa Monica."

"Does it have a rear exit?"

She giggled. "Over the roof. Consuelo said you would use my car."

"Right. Where's it parked?"

"Garage, in the alley."

"You are a gem, my love. Let's get the hell out of here."

Another giggle. "Consuelo said you were a nut."

"Oh, but a rich one."

He paid and they waded through the scowls of the other women to the sidewalk and the Cougar.

"Mitch, my lad, I have found the girl of my dreams. Tell the man where heaven is, my dear, so he can take us there."

Nadine gave him the address and got into the game by tussling with Carter in the back seat all the way there.

"Have a beer if you want to, Mitch," Carter said with a leer. "I'll be a while."

Nadine had the key in her hand and she used it on the inner door with no lost motion. In the hall, a closed door stood on the right and the staircase mounted straight ahead along the left wall. The only light came from a narrow hall that cut toward the front of the house and gave on to the stairs to the floor above.

Nadine unlocked the one at the right and reached in to snap on a wall switch. It was an old-fashioned lock with a big key, and when she had waved Carter ahead of her, she shut the door and locked it from the inside, leaving the key in the lock. This done, she stepped close, put her arms around his waist and smiled.

"Well, what now?"

He slipped away and started checking out the apartment. "Not what you think, darlin'."

She stopped in the middle of pullling her sweater off. "You mean, you really don't want . . ."

Carter was prowling. "Not that you're not adorable . . . but I've got business."

The apartment consisted in the main of one large room. There were two doors on the right, one leading to a long and narrow kitchen, and the other opened on what appeared to be a dressing room and bath. The main room, though sizable, had a cluttered, feminine look. The slipcovers were flowery, worn-looking, and a little cheap. The oversize studio couch that was placed against one wall supported four fancy pillows and a yellow teddy bear. The dressing table next to it held two lamps with pink shades on either side of the mirror, and the beauty aids that littered the top gave it a messy look.

"You at least want a drink?" Nadine asked at his elbow.

"Nope, just the keys to your car and the back way out of here." He peeled off five hundreds and shoved them in her hand.

"My God . . ."

"Five more when I get back," Carter said. "Now, how do I leave?"

"Those windows." She pointed to the two tall windows at the rear of the room. "There's a shed under one of them," she whispered, and took his arm. "Come on."

She beat him to the left-hand window and started to open it. He completed the operation and leaned out to see the shadowy roof not more than five or six feet below him. He started to climb through, then stopped.

"By the way . . ."

"Yeah?"

"Just in case my driver gets curious, you might thrash around on the bed and groan every now and then."

"Sure," she said, grinning, "just me and my teddy bear."

Carter chuckled and, clutching her car keys in his hand, dropped to the shed and then to the ground.

TEN

She parked the rented Ford on the main promenade, the Malecón, and stepped out into the midday heat. She wore a white summer suit and a silk foulard pinned high about her throat. Her bearing, as she crossed the promenade, seemed to defy the heat. Her hair was done primly in a bun at the back of her neck and her eyes were shaded with rose-tinted glasses.

She looked trim, tailored, cool, and professional.

On the opposite sidewalk, she paused. Small shops lined both sides of the walkway leading off the promenade and ending far below at an overlook where diners had a view of the sparkling Pacific.

There was no hesitation in her step as she made for the door of the Joubert Gallery, pushed it open, and entered.

Inside, she found one enormous room. Paintings hung on the walls and sculpture gleamed from pedestals and glass cases.

At the entrance she picked up folders listing the numbers, titles, and asking prices for what was on display and available. Tucking them into the large shoulder bag she carried, she headed toward the rear where a short flight of stairs led to a second level and an office area.

She had just reached the top level when a tall, dark-haired woman emerged from an office and barred her way.

"Good afternoon, I am Marie Joubert. May I help you?" She spoke with a decided French accent.

"Yes, I called you from the airport. I'm the person doing the article on foreign businesses in Mexico." She withdrew a press card from her bag and passed it to the other woman.

"Oh, yes, Miss Royce . . ."

"Trilby, please."

"I'm flattered you think my little business deserves mention in your article."

"Oh, Madame Joubert, I don't think you give yourself enough credit. I understand that you and your husband handle some of the most successful artists in the area, as well as being experts on pre-Columbian artifacts."

Marie Joubert replied with a Gaelic shrug of her well-tailored shoulders. "How may I help you?"

"A short interview perhaps, but first I would like to look the whole gallery over to . . . well, get a feel."

"Of course. This way," the gallery owner replied, smiling as they crossed to her office.

The office was small, the younger woman noted, with an excellent view of the ground floor. She was led through the office to a second door at the far end. When she opened the door they stood on another small flight of stairs above a storage room.

The woman who called herself Trilby Royce smiled when she saw the large doors in the rear of the room that led to an alley behind the gallery.

"I am afraid there isn't much," Marie Joubert said.

"Oh, but I want to see it all, every inch of it."

In the next hour, she had a complete map in her head of the Joubert Gallery, and a brief interview with its owner. During that interview, she informed Marie Joubert that she would be returning in three days' time from Mazatlán. Could she have the pleasure of taking Madame Joubert to lunch?"

"Friday? Oh, no, I am afraid that would be impossible. I have a client coming in from ten in the morning until sometime in the afternoon on Friday."

"You must stay in the shop for a single client?"

Madame Joubert chuckled and leaned forward confidentially. "*This* client I handle myself. In fact, he is so important that we close the shop while he is here."

The woman took up no more of Madame Joubert's valuable time.

Besides, she had found out everything she wanted to know.

Carter stood in the lobby, smoking, waiting until the crowd returning from late lunches thinned. When there was only a trickle of people coming through the big doors and no one was pausing at the newsstand, he approached.

"Hello, Kurt."

The short, bald-headed man behind the counter smiled at the voice, his sightless eyes behind the lightly tinted glasses unmoving. "Hello yourself."

"Just thought I'd check and see if you got those back issues of *Playboy* I ordered."

"Sure thing." The head disappeared beneath the counter. "Let's see now . . . how many issues was that?"

"Twenty," Carter replied.

A sealed cardboard box came over the counter. "There you are . . . Nick, isn't it?"

"That's right."

"Thirty-seven-eighty."

Carter gave him a fifty, and was amazed when it was identified by feel only and the change made.

"By the way, Nick, I heard from your aunt."

"Oh?"

"Yeah. She wants you to call. That friend you've been trying to locate . . ."

"Yes?"

"She thinks she may have found him."

"Thanks, Kurt, thanks a lot."

"Any time."

Carter had parked Nadine's beat-up Pontiac in the darkest corner of the underground garage. When he reached it, he tore open the carton. The top two magazines were intact. The eighteen below them had been gutted in the center to hide the fat money belt.

When Carter had it secured around his middle and his shirt back in his pants, he headed for the Harbor Freeway and Long Beach.

California Dreamin' wasn't exactly a rust bucket, but it would never make devotees of the America's Cup quiver with the desire for ownership.

Carter paused on the dockside of the narrow gangway and jiggled a boatswain's bell hanging across a guard rope with his knee. Even the sound from the bell seemed dull.

"Ahoy, *California Dreamin'*, may I come aboard?"

The rear hatch came up, paused, and slammed against the deck, spraying paint chips.

"Depends what the hell ya want!"

If she had been a man she could have played for the Lakers. Carter guessed her at around six-three, and thought even as a woman she could probably play for the Lakers.

All she wore was a tiny black string bikini that scarcely made an effort to contain what it held. Carter moved a step forward and visualized the twin Trade Towers in lower Manhattan on their sides.

He guessed her a year or two above twenty, with a hard face and very little sense of humor. But she did have a lot of everything else, a rich, heavy spill of honey-blond hair, exercise-honed thighs, and a sleek, deeply tanned torso.

"Is Rocco around?"

"He's sleepin' off a drunk."

"Swell."

"Who wants him?"

"I have an appointment," Carter said, moving forward until he stepped on the deck.

"Bullshit. Rocco never made an appointment in his life."

Her attitude was starting to rankle. Carter moved forward another step. "Look, lady, are you his bodyguard . . . ?"

Suddenly, Carter's right arm was being yanked out of its socket. A well-curved hip caught him dead center in the gut and he saw the mane of honey-blond hair below instead of above him. Then he hit the deck flat on his back and a sturdy knee was in his throat.

Above him, the Amazon was smiling. "I think you're a smartass."

Carter started to roll, but killed the move quickly when the thumb of his right hand was twisted down to touch his wrist.

"Steady," she hissed.

"You blind-sided me," Carter growled.

"No shit."

Suddenly there was a roar from belowdecks. "What the hell's goin' on up there?"

"Dude says he wants to talk to ya."

"What's his name?"

"What's your name?"

"Nick, and if you don't get your knee out of my throat, I'm going to break your leg."

Footsteps sounded on the ladder and one half of a hairy ape in boxer shorts appeared in the hatch opening. "Let him up, Godiva."

Immediately the girl sprung clear and Carter sat up rubbing his throat. "Rocco Parks?"

The reply was an affirmative nod.

Rocco Parks had a good smile even though it involved only his mouth. He was short, with a sleek cap of black hair that matched the fur that literally covered his body. He was broad-shouldered, slim-hipped, and muscled like a weight lifter. He wore only the boxer shorts, and ropes of muscle crawled under his skin when he moved.

"Tough, ain't she?" Parks asked with a grin.

"Yeah," Carter said, glancing at the Amazon. "But she cheats."

This brought a chuckle that sounded like a growl from Parks's throat. "Me and him got some talkin' to do, Godiva. Go do some grocery shoppin' fer an hour."

"What the hell do we need?"

"What we always need," Parks roared. "Scotch, gin, vodka, beer! Move!"

Godiva adjusted her breasts in their minute hammocks and hit the pier. Carter followed the other man below.

"Beer?"

Carter nodded and brought up what he knew about

Rocco Parks in his memory bank. He had been a champion amateur boxer, and with his desire, ability, killer instinct, and size, he could have been, possibly, champion of the world, professionally, in his weight class. Except he had bad hands. After he'd broken his right hand for the ninth or tenth time, he'd hung up the gloves.

With the money he had saved, he bought the boat and took fishermen out by the day. He had come to AXE's attention a few years earlier when they had needed someone to infiltrate a ring of dopers in Mexico bringing Chinese white into the States.

Since then Parks had been used several times, and his ratings were high, as were his prices.

Carter took the Mexican beer and matched his host swallow for swallow. Parks's eyes, green and yellow like a coyote's, gleamed at Carter over the bottle.

"Okay, what's the deal? The call I got said a week."

Carter nodded. "Give or take a day or two. You know the Mexican coast?"

"Every inch of it."

"I need to get into Puerto Vallarta sight unseen. When the job's done, I'll need to get out the same way."

Parks nodded. "Can do."

"We'll also need a cove or something to cool off for a day or two."

"Know just the place. How many besides yourself?"

"Two . . . man and woman," Carter replied.

Parks finished his beer and popped the cap off of another. "It'll be tight, but no problem. When do we leave?"

"Tonight, the wee hours." Carter pulled a notebook from his pocket and tore out a page. "Can you get these extras?"

Parks scanned the list and frowned. "The hardware, easy. The plastique may take a little time."

"How much time?"

Rocco Parks grinned. "At least three hours."

Carter returned the grin and then dropped it. "Who's Godiva?"

"A lady wrestler."

"That figures. How does she fit here, though?"

"She's my first mate."

"Can you leave her here?"

"I can," Parks replied, "but I won't."

Carter mulled this over, remembered how she had taken him topside, and decided not to argue. "When we move, it has to be fast. Be ready to leave anytime after midnight."

"Done. Now, it's a thousand a day and yer little list here is extra."

Carter pulled his shirt from his pants to reveal the money belt. He emptied five of the pouches and piled the bills on the table between them. "That should more than cover the whole trip."

Park's fingers did a Yellow-Pages walk to the bills. "Love doin' business with you people, love it!"

Carter returned to the Pontiac and headed north. A few blocks short of Nadine's apartment, he pulled into a convenience store and used the outside pay phone.

"Trilby?"

"Where the hell have you been?" she cried from the other end of the line. "I'm in prison down here!"

"You're about to be sprung."

He brought her up to date and gave her an approximate pickup time. Then he hung up before he got any more static.

The second call was to Washington, and he had to

wait nearly two minutes before Ginger Bateman came on the line.

"Hello, Auntie, this is your loving nephew. What have you got?"

"A bombshell, maybe. The office that wants you so bad is NSA-Pentagon liaison."

Carter whistled. "That's up there. Got a name?"

"Two, actually. A major who filed the initial request, and a civilian secretary who sent them out. We're working quietly on the secretary, but the major suddenly went on leave when we started digging."

"Stay on it," Carter said, "and check out a Colonel Jeffrey Cornwall. He's probably in Lisbon, and he may be a brigadier by now."

"Will do. When do you move?"

"Tonight, so I might not be able to contact back until it's over."

Carter hung up and drove the rest of the way to Nadine's. He parked in the tiny garage, and after making sure there were no snoopy neighbors, made the climb to the woman's rear window.

He was just coming through the window when Nadine emerged from the bathroom toweling drops of water from her lush curves.

"Am I glad you're back," she said frowning. "I've taken a shower for you, a shower for me, and I've about groaned myself hoarse on that damn bed."

She was whispering and Carter did the same. "Problems?"

"Your driver. He's been up here twice. Knocked on the door, said he wanted to make sure you weren't getting rolled."

Carter smiled. "I'll bet. What did you tell him?"

"The first time I said you were passed out. The second

time, just a few minutes ago, you were in the shower. I think he's out there in the hall right now, prowling around.''

Carter took the roll out of his pocket and peeled off another five hundred.

Nadine looked at the bills in her hand and then up at him with a narrow-eyed squint. ''Bull.''

''Bull what?''

''This doesn't add up. A grand to play with myself and take a couple of showers?''

Carter put his hands on each side of her face and kissed her gently on the lips. ''You've been a big help. And you're right . . . there's more to all this than I'm telling you. Now, do us both a favor. Take the grand and get out of town for a few days. I'm going to tell your sister the same thing tonight. Okay?''

She swallowed hard. ''Okay. I've got a boyfriend in San Diego.''

Carter kissed her again. ''The two of you have a ball . . . on me.''

In the bathroom he dampened his hair an ran a comb through it. When he came back into the main room, Nadine was sitting, still naked, on the bed, staring at the pile of bills in her lap.

''Like I said,'' Carter quipped, ''don't try to figure it out.''

ELEVEN

A little snooping and Carter found out that Tall-and-Handsome and Plump-and-Redheaded were Mr. and Mrs. Raymond Justice. He scouted the bar, the beach, and the pool, but he didn't see them.

From the lobby pay phone, he called the desk. "Yeah, put me through to Ray Justice, please—this is long distance. He's in Suite Ten-twelve."

"No, sir, that's Bungalow F. I'll ring."

"Thanks."

The voice that answered had a British accent. "Yes, what is it?"

Carter held his nose. "Room service, Mr. Justice. I think we've got a mix-up here. Did you just ring for cocktails?"

"I did not."

"Sorry."

The Killmaster hung up and went into the concession shop across the way. He bought a can of lighter fluid, pocketed it, and headed out across the pool area. In the gardens he turned right to the row of bungalows that fronted the beach. Bungalow F was the fifth one in a line, and all of the drapes were drawn.

Carter hugged the door and knocked.

"Yes?"

"Room service, sir."

The door swung wide. "I just told the chap on the phone—"

Carter nailed him from the side, flush on his right ear, and Justice went to one knee. Carter shoved him back into the room with a foot in the center of the chest, stepped into the bungalow, and closed the door behind him.

The guy was in swimming trunks and he was no shrimp. He bunched the muscles in his big shoulders and came off the floor to ram his head into Carter's gut.

Carter nailed him again, cupping the palm of his left hand across the same ear. The concussive force of the air driven against the eardrum jerked a whistling grunt of pain from the man's throat. His hands came up and his head twisted aside in agony.

Carter stepped in, set his right foot, and buried his fist in Justice's gut. A follow-up left on the point of the chin drove him back against the wall where he folded like a burnt match.

The Killmaster checked the kitchen, bedroom, and bath. No little woman. He found her undies in a drawer and selected a handful of panties, three pair of panty hose, and a bra.

Back in the sitting room, Justice was fighting for air and consciousness.

Carter used a pair of panty hose each on the ankles and wrists, and attached them. Then he looped the crotch of the third pair around the man's neck and attached it to his wrists in the small of his back. If Justice struggled too much to free himself, he would choke to death.

The panties Carter stuffed in the man's mouth as a gag, and secured them with the bra knotted tightly at the back of his head.

As a last touch, he ripped apart the man's swimming trunks and threw them across the room. A naked man with it all hanging out develops an inferiority complex that sometimes makes him talk faster.

Carter moved back into the bedroom. The man's wallet, his passport, and about two thousand in cash lay on top of the dresser. The wallet said he was Raymond Justice, age forty-one, and according to a driver's license about to expire, he lived in Baltimore.

The passport was a little more revealing. According to the last set of entry-and-exit stamps, Justice had entered Portugal four months earlier and stayed there until only a week ago. There was an international driver's license tucked into the back of the passport, with an issue date on it about two weeks before the entry date on the passport into Portugal.

Back in the living room, Justice's eyes were bulging and his face was darkening from lack of air. Saliva was dripping from the corners of his mouth around the panties and dribbling down his chin.

Carter knelt in front of him and stared at the plea in the man's eyes, the kicking legs, and the straining shoulder muscles.

"Can you hear and understand me? Nod!"

Fierce hatred in the eyes and no movement of the head.

Carter backhanded him, hard, across the face, and the head started nodding as if it were on a string.

"I'm going to take the gag out, but don't breathe. If you breathe, you'll aspirate into your lungs and have pneumonia by five o'clock. Got that?"

More nodding.

Carter rolled him facedown onto the floor and untied the bra. When he jerked the panties from Justice's mouth, he hit him hard in the center of the back. The results of Carter's gut-punch spewed out onto the carpet and in a couple of minutes the man was breathing normally.

"Oh, God . . . sick, I'm sick," Justice gasped.

"Shit, friend," Carter rasped, "you don't know sick yet."

He rolled the man back to a seated position and again knelt in front of him. "Where's the little woman?"

"Out."

"I can see that. Out where?"

"Hairdresser's. Look here, I don't know who you are . . ."

Carter smiled. "You mean you didn't know who I was until I walked through that door. Now we're going to play twenty questions, and if you want to keep your manhood, you'll answer every one of them right on the nose. We'll start with something easy. Who do you work for?"

Justice lunged forward, trying to butt Carter with his head. The Killmaster twisted aside and jerked his knee up into Justice's face. With a howl of pain and his nose spurting blood, he tried to rise for another go, but he could only get to his knees.

Now Carter decided to really get rough. He laughed aloud, got to his feet, and grabbed a handful of the salt-and-pepper hair. He jerked Justice's face down, and at the same time drove his knee a second time into the handsome face.

"I can keep this up a long time, Justice, so long even your own mother wouldn't know you when I'm through."

He lifted Justice's head and brought his knee into position to drive it up again.

"No, no, please, enough . . ."

Carter paused with the knee but kept his grip on the hair. "You want to try me again? How about it?"

"No more, no more, please!"

"So you say now. I don't think you're quite convinced."

"You're crazy, a crazy bastard! What do you want?"

"I already asked. Who do you work for?"

"The government, foreign service."

"And you're currently attached to the embassy in Portugal." Justice looked surprised. "Your passport is diplomatic. What brings you to California?"

"Loretta and I are on holiday."

"Loretta's the little woman?"

Justice nodded. "She's a military analyst. We're stationed together at the embassy is Lisbon."

"So far, so good," Carter growled. "What do you do for Comrex?"

"Comrex? I don't know anything about Comrex."

Carter shook his head and gave the man a world-weary smile. "Raymond, my boy, you are so frigging stupid. I'm a pro and you are in over your ass."

The Killmaster gave him a long ten seconds to come up with an answer. When he didn't, Carter got to his feet and walked to the glass doors that led to the rear patio. They were decorated with little butterfly decals so that guests under the influence wouldn't walk through them on the way to the pool.

The bungalows were all top-drawer. Each of them had its own small pool and enclosed patio.

He opened the glass door but left the screen door latched, and returned to Justice.

The man was frightened and bewildered. He was still not actually aware that he was stark naked. Carter dragged him to his feet and across the room. Five feet from the patio exit, Carter sent him sailing through the screened door. The wire parted like bacon sizzling, and Justice sailed end over end across the patio with Carter right behind him.

The Killmaster rolled him over and over with well-placed kicks until the man slid into the pool. He tried to shout, but water filled his mouth, cutting off his cry as he sank.

Carter went to the side of the pool and looked down into the clear water. Justice kicked and lunged trying to fight his way back to the top and life, up where the air was. He made it, throwing his head back, mouth open and gasping. Carter put his foot on Justice's head and shoved him back under.

Twice more when Justice surfaced, Carter let him get just enough air to give him hope, and sent him down again. When Justice quit making bubbles and stopped struggling and came slowly floating to the top, Carter grabbed a handful of hair and towed him facedown, turned his face to the side, then pounded on Justice's back with the side of his right fist. In a few moments Justice stirred, opened his eyes, saw Carter, shut his eyes, and shook his head.

"I'm dying . . . you're killing me . . ."

"Not quite, but almost," the Killmaster hissed. "Who's your immediate superior in Comrex?"

The swollen eyes came up and weighed Carter. They flickered and the jaw set. At that moment Carter knew he wasn't going to get anything substantial out of the man.

"I talk, they kill me. I don't talk, you kill me." He shrugged. "Go to hell."

Wearily, Carter yanked the panty hose tight against the man's carotid artery. In seconds Justice was out cold.

He wrapped his hand around Justice's arm just above the elbow, lifted, and dragged him back through the living room into the bedroom.

When the panty gag was back in his mouth and secure, Carter went over the bungalow again. The only item he unearthed that he had missed earlier was a spare clip for a .25 automatic. Because of the caliber, and the fact that he couldn't find the gun, it was a good guess that it was in little Loretta's purse.

This gave Carter another piece of interesting intelligence. If the lady was packing and her husband wasn't, then it was probably Loretta Justice and not Raymond who had the final order on Carter if they found him.

He got a fresh supply of panty hose and went through the bungalow extinguishing all the lights. This done, he settled back to wait.

It wasn't long, twenty minutes, when he heard the *tap, tap, tap* of her heels on the walk.

He took her just as she came through the door. "Ray . . . did you go back to bed . . . ?"

He wasn't gentle. He flipped a noose of nylon over her head, jammed the knot tight against her neck under the ear across the carotid, and kicked her feet from her. In fifteen seconds she was unconscious.

He picked her up, carried her into the bedroom, threw her on the king-size bed beside her husband, loosened the knot so blood could get to her brain, and then stripped her.

Each time she seemed to come back almost to full consciousness, Carter tightened the noose and she went out again. He stretched her full length and tied her hands above her head, her feet to the footboard.

He loosened the knot and let her come back all the way, helping her by dumping melting ice wrapped in a towel on her belly. After a moment, he moved the lumpy towel up between her vast breasts and used an end to wipe her face.

She shook so hard with fear, and perhaps with cold, that Carter could feel the bed tremble against his leg. When she looked to her left and saw her husband lying there like a roped calf, she gasped, slung her head back and forth, and tried to scream. But nothing would come; all she could make was a thin whine.

"Can you hear me, Loretta?"

"Wh-who . . . are . . . you?"

"Can you hear? Do you understand?"

"My *God,* what's going on?"

Carter found her purse and lifted the little Beretta .25 automatic from it. It was definitely a woman's gun, but up close it could be just as deadly as a Howitzer.

He returned to the bed and looked down at her, smiling, holding the gun above her face with two fingers. "Hi, Loretta. I'm the guy you were going to use this on."

Her face was already a little gray; now it went stark white. She took another gander at her husband, gave him up for dead, and stared back at Carter.

"Want to tell me about Comrex, Loretta? Who gave you your orders in Lisbon to take a holiday in California? Who runs you here? That's for starters." He pulled up a chair and sat beside the bed. "Old Ray over there decided that I was the lesser of two evils. He told me to go ahead and kill him. What do you say, Loretta?"

Her eyes flashed. "I am an employee of the United States government. I don't know who you are, but—"

"Oh, shit, Loretta."

Carter took the can of lighter fluid from his pocket and moved to the head of the bed. He sprayed her right hand with the fluid and snapped his lighter until it flamed.

"My God, you're a sadist!" she cried.

"No, Loretta, a realist." He touched the lighter to the right hand and it immediately burst into flames.

Loretta's back arched and her eyes rolled up, showing a rim of white. For the first few seconds the yellow flame tipped with blue didn't harm her, only burned, and she watched with terrified fascination. Then the excess fluid burned away and the fire began to eat into her flesh. She screamed.

Carter jammed his hand over her mouth. She tried to bite him. He slapped her, hard. He took a handful of panty hose and jammed them into her mouth. He sprayed her hand again and lit it. She bucked and fought the nylon bindings of her own panty hose that tied her to the bed. Carter put the fire out, slapping the flames away with his hand. Her hand was puckered with burn blisters, none serious.

He sat down in the chair and took the wadded nylon from her mouth. "Loretta, I'm only going to say this once. Do you hear me?"

"Yes."

"Then listen. If you don't tell me everything I want to know, I am going to melt you."

For emphasis he emptied the can of lighter fluid over her body, starting at her breasts and moving all the way to her toes. Then he held up the lighter.

"One touch, Loretta, and *poof,* up you go."

She talked. Oh my, how she talked.

Colonel Jeffery Cornwall had recruited them nearly five years earlier. There were two lures, money and strident nationalism. The whole operation was broken into cells. No one individual cell knew the leaders or the members of the others.

Cornwall wasn't the big gun, but he was high in the

chain of command. A man by the name of Wynne had been their control since their arrival in the States. Loretta didn't know who he was, but she was pretty sure he was high up, maybe had access to the very top man himself. He worked with someone named Cruz, but he, Wynne, was the top gun.

It was the Justice's job to spot Carter when he tried to contact Josh Royce. Wynne would do the actual hit, but she and her husband would provide backup.

"Who was supposed to take out Royce and his daughter?"

"No one."

"What?"

"No one," Loretta repeated, her eyes on the lighter Carter kept playing with. "I swear it. Wynne even said that if we spotted you with Royce or the girl, we were to lay off until we got you alone."

Carter paced, digested this wrinkle in his mind, and went on.

"Does Comrex have some kind of central headquarters?"

"I don't know," she gasped. Carter flicked the lighter. "I don't, I swear it! But since we've been in Portugal I've delivered pouches to a place in the mountains about twenty miles inland from Sintra. It's called Castillo Augustine."

"What was in the pouches?"

"I think money . . . lots of it."

"One more thing, Loretta. Names . . . I want the names of everyone in Comrex you've come in contact with since you were recruited."

The list was impressive. Carter stored each name away as she spouted it. She would have gone on for another hour, but the Killmaster was pretty sure he had enough for the AXE research people to get some kind of a link.

He pocketed the lighter and the empty fluid can, then got together more underwear for Loretta's gag.

"Listen," she pleaded, "don't do that. If they find us like this, they'll know we talked. They'll kill us, I swear! Let us go. We'll run."

Carter gazed down at her calmly. "Where can you run to, Loretta?"

That one stumped her. Before she could put together another appeal, he fastened the gag and left the bungalow.

As he locked the door he took the DO NOT DISTURB sign and hung it on the outside knob.

Consuelo Cortez cut her second show short by twenty minutes. When they reached her bungalow, Carter noticed that she was already packed and ready to go.

She was elated but didn't seem too surprised when he laid a whole thousand on her and, as he'd done with her sister, suggested a vacation.

"Out of curiosity," she said, "am I doing all this for a good cause? Because your story about a married girlfriend smells."

"A very good cause," Carter replied, and made for the patio door.

Louise Girard was waiting in the same car she had used the previous night. Carter was scarcely in the rear seat when she took off.

"It's on Ocean Boulevard, The Pelican's Roost."

"I'll find it," she said.

Carter turned to Royce and relayed everything he had learned from little Loretta.

Two facts got a big rise out of Royce: the Portugal connection, and Wynne.

"That would be Cal Wynne. He was one of the American overseers for the CIA's Air America in 'Nam. Through them he did some supplying for Phoenix Force when they worked in Laos and Cambodia."

"That was then," Carter growled. "What about now?"

Royce's face looked grim. "He went into the FBI when he left the service. The last I heard, he was the Bureau's main link with the Drug Enforcement Administration."

Carter nodded. "That would give him a lot of leeway. What about Portugal? It seems all roads lead there."

Royce nodded and sighed. "It would seem so. I had a theory once, but it was a little farfetched. That's why I never mentioned it."

"Well, mention it now," Carter said, lighting up and dragging deep.

"Angola," Royce said. "As near as I can figure, Comrex got its first real foothold right after the Cubans went in to help the rebels there."

"That would figure," Carter said. "A lot of Portuguese VIPs lost their butts when Portugal lost Angola as a colony. If Comrex got to those people, it would be a good start."

"There's your Pelican," Louise Girard said from the front seat.

"Pull around to the corner," Carter replied, "to the mouth of the alley."

The Killmaster was out of the car and moving before it came to a complete stop. He darted up the alley and vaulted a low brick wall that surrounded the pool.

There was a single light in front and no lights by the pool. The drapes of every room were pulled tight, so only dim light gleamed through tiny cracks. One of the rooms with lights on was Trilby's.

Carter knocked.

"Yes?" came a cautious voice from the other side of the door.

"It's me."

"Who's me?"

"Dammit, Trilby, open the door!"

It opened a crack and he slid through. She came immediately into his arms. "Nick, the police were here!"

"What?"

"Cops, local cops. They had a picture of me. I'm supposed to be wanted for questioning. The woman who runs the place saw them go to three other motels up the line."

"What happened?"

Trilby smiled. "The woman told them she had never seen me. Then she came back and told me." The smile faded. "She also said she could easily change her mind."

"How much?" Carter growled.

"I gave her a little over two hundred dollars. It was all I had."

"Good move. Now, c'mon, let's get out of here."

Outside, he boosted her over the rear wall and they ran for the car. All the while, Carter's mind was racing.

Josh Royce wasn't kidding when he said they had tapped into the police computers.

TWELVE

The trip south was no problem. Rocco Parks turned out to be one hell of a seaman. Carter even made his peace with Godiva, who also turned out to be a good sailor.

If the *California Dreamin'* looked like hell on the surface, she was quite the opposite in her innards. Twin 300-horsepower Chrysler marines drove her down the coast at speeds up to sixty knots per hour. Once in a while, when other boats looked inquisitive, Parks would slow down and they would throw out the lines.

Just after dawn, Rocco nudged Carter and took him below. In the forward cabin he reached under the decks, around a bilge pump, and drew out a thick oilskin package. With pride he unwrapped it and hefted one of the rifles in his hands.

"M-11 Ingram machine pistol. Weighs about four pounds, fires eight hundred and fifty rounds a minute, and uses thirty-eight-caliber shells. Two of 'em, and I got six spare clips for each."

Carter grinned. "Rocco, you live up to your reputation.'' He hefted two of the three Colt .45s from the bag. ''Loaded?''

Parks nodded. ''And a spare clip for each. The plastique is in caps like you said, with quick fuses.''

''Let's hope we don't need it,'' Royce said.

''Yeah,'' Carter agreed, nodding, ''let's hope. What about the car and the clothes?''

''Godiva will take care of that when we get there. I've already made a couple of calls. There are several villas north of Puerto Vallarta. The owners keep a car in the garage to use when they come down. A guy named Manuel is a gardener. He's spotting one for us now.''

Under cover of darkness, they slid into a little cove that was perfect to hide the boat. They were barely rocking at anchor when Godiva was in the skiff and gone.

She was back in two hours, and dropped a set of keys in Carter's hand.

''It's a blue Toyota parked in a cutout about halfway up the cliff. Clothes are in the trunk.''

''When do you go?'' Parks asked.

''First thing in the morning,'' Carter replied. ''Let's all get some sleep.''

''General?''

''Yes, Wynne?''

''We're ready to move. We can't delay or some of Aldami's people are liable to get suspicious.''

''I am leaving for Lisbon this afternoon. Everything is ready there. I don't want a delay. Go.''

''But, General,'' Wynne said, ''what if Royce doesn't show up?''

There was a chuckle from the other end of the line. ''We've made an ID on the agent Royce contacted. He discovered the Justice couple."

"I was afraid that might happen," Wynne grumbled.

"Not to worry, my boy. The agent's name is Carter. He will only add weight to our little plan, if you see my point."

Wynne smiled. "Indeed I do. And Raymond Justice?"

"He and his ambitious wife have been taken care of."

"I'll report to Lisbon as soon as we're in the clear," Wynne said, and hung up.

He moved out of the little cantina. It was hot on the street. People clogged the sidewalks, looking in stores. Most were in shorts or swimsuits and on their way to or from the beach.

Wynne walked a few blocks farther into the new town. Cruz was parked on a side street under a large tree.

"So?" he said when Wynne slid into the car.

"I just walked by the shop. The Mexican girl is starting to get rid of the customers."

Cruz nodded and tapped the walkie in his lap. "Aldami and his bodyguards have left the yacht. They're on the way in. All our other people are in place."

"All right, it's a go."

Marie Joubert watched as her assistant, Enriqueta, ushered the last customer out of the shop. The girl turned the CLOSED/CERRADO sign outward and locked the door.

"That's fine, Enriqueta," Marie said. "Set up the stands for the more expensive pieces, and then come up and have a sandwich with me."

"*Sí, señora*. Should I put the front alarm on?"

"No need. Monsieur Aldami and his entourage should be here within the hour."

"*Sí, señora*."

Marie Joubert was about to sit back down at her desk, when she heard a light tapping sound from the storage room. At first she paid no attention, but when it came again she put down her sandwich, entered the room, and went down the steps.

The tapping came again. It was on the loading dock door.

"Damn," she said aloud, "I have nothing coming in today."

Reaching up, she switched off the alarm for the rear of the gallery, took out her keys, and unlocked the door.

There were three of them with black ski masks over their faces. Her surprise at seeing them delayed the scream from reaching her lips.

By then it was too late. The chloroform in the pad over her face had done its work.

Carter turned off the main road into the old town. He wound through the street and eventually drove by the gallery.

"There's an alley," Royce said.

Carter had already spotted it. Near the loading dock entrance to the rear of the gallery, a Lincoln Continental with Mexican plates was parked.

"Must belong to the couple that owns the place," Royce said. "Park here, on the street."

Carter pulled to the nose of the alley and parked. In the rearview mirror he could see Trilby just taking a table in the café across from the front of the gallery.

"Josh, are you sure she can use that forty-five?"

"She can handle it. I taught her myself."

"That's what I'm afraid of," Carter said dryly.

Both of them were dressed in the baggy white trousers, dirty white shirts, and wide-brimmed straw hats worn by

Mexican farmers. The skin on their faces and hands had been darkened, and the serapes over their shoulders hid the Ingrams.

"Okay," Carter said, "let's walk the perimeter and find out how many and where they are."

In the office of the gallery, Wynne thumbed the button of his walkie. "Harris, where are they?"

"Just getting off the launch. Besides Aldami, there are four. They have a black Cadillac limo waiting. ETA to you should be about twenty minutes."

"Check," Wynne said. "Cruz?"

"I'm on the roof at the end of the street. I can see front and back."

"Any sign of Royce and this Carter?"

"None so far."

"Damn, keep your eyes open."

"Check."

Wynne moved to the door. The Mexican girl placed a ceramic figurine on the last vacant stand and headed toward the stairs.

"Got 'em?" Carter growled.

"Yeah," Royce answered. "Only two. One window-shopping down there, the other haggling with that taco vendor."

"That's it," Carter said. "The others must be inside already. Let's go."

Carter and Royce turned into the alley and sprinted toward the loading dock door. The Killmaster already had a lockpick in his hands, but the door was unlocked.

"I'll take this end," Royce said. "You take the front."

"Right," Carter said, and kept going.

• • •

Wynne lowered the Mexican girl to the floor just as the walkie on his belt came to life. The odor of chloroform was heavy in the air.

"Wynne?"

"Yeah, go ahead, Cruz."

"I think I've got 'em. They're dressed like *campesinos*. One of 'em is coming in the loading door; the other's heading for the street."

"Got it," Wynne said, and turned to look back into the office.

One of the two "men" had stripped off his outer layer of dark clothing and removed the ski mask. What emerged was a tall blonde in dark slacks and a white blouse.

"Are you ready, Isabel?"

The woman fluffed her blond hair and put on a pair of dark glasses. "Ready."

"Then go!"

She slipped a magnum into the belt of her slacks at the small of her back and started down the stairs.

"Eddie," Wynne growled, "take out the one coming in the loading door."

"You got it," said the other man, and took up a place at the top of the stairs just as the loading door below him began to open.

Wynne turned back. He could see Bevello Aldami step out of the limousine. Three bodyguards accompanied him across the sidewalk.

Isabel unlocked the door as the chauffeur lounged against a front fender and lit a cigarette.

Aldami was scarcely inside the front door when the woman put her shoulder to his side and sent him sprawling to the floor. At the same time, she deftly drew the magnum and shot two of the bodyguards.

From the balcony, Wynne shot the third guard three times in the chest. Behind him he heard Eddie open up with the shotgun.

The woman leaped over the two bodies and aimed. Both of the magnum slugs hit the limo driver in the chest. He tumbled into the street, dead when he hit the pavement.

Josh Royce was moving cautiously up the steps when he heard the first shot from the front of the gallery. Just as he broke into a run up the remainder of the steps he saw movement above him.

Too late, he brought up the Ingram.

Both barrels from the shotgun hit him in the center of the chest. He was dead before he hit the loading dock behind him.

Just as Carter hit the front corner of the building, he knew he was too late. He heard the dull thump of a magnum, twice, and then the chatter of an automatic rifle.

He was throwing off the serape and bringing up the Ingram, when everything happened at once.

A shotgun went off inside the gallery. A body tumbled through the front door. The magnum barked again and the limo driver sprawled into the street.

People were screaming and running everywhere in the streets. The front of the gallery was out. Carter couldn't see inside before those inside could see him.

He ran back to the loading dock door and charged through. He did a roll and came up on one knee. Two black-clad figures were at the top of the stiars. One of them had a walkie up to the ski mask over his face.

Carter cut loose with the Ingram. Because he had to

dive at the same time, he knew he had missed. The crate behind where he had been exploded from the double barrels of the shotgun.

He heard the barrel click open, and darted out for another burst. The one with the walkie had hung it on his belt and come up with a rifle.

Again Carter couldn't get a decent shot. Slugs from the rifle were dancing inches from his body. He kept rolling until he found more crates to dive behind.

He saw Josh Royce when he came to a stop. He was on his back, the serape blown clear off his body, his bloody chest enough to tell Carter he was gone.

"Let's go! We got one of them, that's enough!"

The voice came from directly above Carter, and was quickly followed by the sound of running feet.

Carter jumped out from behind the crates. When he drew no fire, he ran for the stairs. He climbed the steps three at a time and burst through the office, making straight for the window that looked out onto the street.

A blond woman was already at the wheel of the limousine. The two hooded figures were pushing a third man into the rear seat. Carter assumed that would be Aldami.

The limo screamed off, and the Lincoln that had been parked in the alley appeared right behind it.

Chase car, Carter thought grimly; *we wouldn't have a chance.*

He ran back down the stairs and tossed the Ingram behind some crates after wiping it clean of prints.

The alley was still deserted. He ran to the Toyota and dived into the driver's seat. At the corner he slowed and turned down toward the main street.

He was nearly to the corner when he spotted Trilby.

She saw him at the same time and bolted from the door of the café.

"What happened . . . it was all so fast . . ."

"Get in."

"Where's Josh?"

"Get in."

"Where's my father?"

Carter opened the door, grabbed her wrist, and yanked her inside. Her butt was barely in the seat when he floored the little car.

"Where's Josh, Nick?"

"He's gone, Trilby. He's gone."

She was stunned into silence all the way to the overlook where Carter parked the car. Quickly he wiped the prints from every conceivable place his fingers could have touched.

"He's dead?" she asked when Carter grabbed her arm.

"Yes, Trilby, he's dead. Just like we're gonna be if we don't move."

It was another two miles to the cove. They covered it at a jog, and ran the last hundred feet down the cliff to the *California Dreamin'*.

Rocco Parks must have seen them coming. The twin Chryslers were already humming.

"Trouble?" he asked when Carter hit the deck.

"A bellyful, and I don't think we can run."

"We might not have to," Parks said. "Have her strip down and stretch out on the cabin roof with Godiva."

Carter looked up. The Amazon was on the cabin roof, stark naked and basting her body with suntan lotion. He got the picture and turned to Trilby.

"Strip."

She just stared back at him. Carter wasted no time.

He ripped the clothes from her body, picked her up in a fireman's carry, and toted her to the roof. Gently he sat her beside Godiva.

"Take care of her."

Godiva nodded. Rocco Parks already had the boat moving when Carter leaped back to the deck.

"Get a couple of fishing poles set up in the stern. Open some beer. I'm only going out about a mile. Get some lines over when I throttle down."

Carter nodded and went to work.

They had been settled in for about five minutes when the police launch came up alongside.

Most Mexican cops asked for their bite and then did their duty or went on about their business.

These three couldn't have cared less about a bribe. They came over the side with guns drawn, and barely looked at the naked flesh on the cabin roof.

One of them started tossing questions while the other two searched. Twenty minutes later they were satisfied that the foursome were just fishermen and sunbathers.

They didn't even say *adiós* as they jumped into their launch and went in pursuit of another boat about a mile up the coast.

THIRTEEN

The tiny television flickered, but it told the story only too well. Bevello Aldami had been kidnapped. All four of his bodyguards were brutally murdered. A fourth victim, assumed to be killed by the bodyguards, had been identified as a CIA agent, Josh Royce.

According to the gallery owner, Madame Marie Joubert, a woman who identified herself as Trilby Royce visited her at the Puerto Vallarta gallery two days earlier. Police are speculating that Miss Royce was in on the plot and visited the gallery to set up the kidnapping.

Madame Joubert's assistant also heard one of the kidnappers address the woman as Trilby, and also heard the name Carter from the woman before she was chloroformed.

"Very neat," Carter hissed, leaning over and snapping off the set.

"How so?" Rocco Parks asked.

Carter lit a cigarette before replying. He remembered little Loretta's comment about Wynne wanting only him, Carter. It was hands-off Trilby and Josh Royce. It was ten to one that Comrex wanted Josh Royce in Puerto Vallarta.

"We were set up, Rocco," he said. "At least, Josh was set up."

"The State Department is going to fry on this one. They say there are already repercussions. Something about the U.S. stepping out of line again to meddle in another country's business."

"Yeah, I'll bet," Carter growled.

He looked up the cliff and saw Trilby in the fading light. Groaning, he got to his feet and dived into the water. He did a lazy crawl to the sand and then walked up the path until he was beside her.

"Trilby?" he murmured gently.

"What?"

"I'm sorry."

"Me, too." She moved toward the edge of the cliff and stared down at the ocean. "What will you do?"

"I gave everything I could to my people in Washington. They have the research people and the computers going full blast. If they can come up with a pattern that gives us the top gun, I'll go after him."

The usual evening breeze came in off the ocean, jiggling the sparse leaves on the trees around them. Carter eyed her beside him and decided to tell her the truth, or at least his guess of it.

"Trilby, Josh was set up, and I think you were meant to go down with him."

Alarm and disbelief registered on her face.

"Hear me out."

He told her about the woman passing herself off as Trilby Royce, using Trilby's press card. He explained that the kidnappers were ready for Josh and himself, literally expecting them. This was borne out by what he had learned from Loretta Justice.

Trilby listened and, to her credit, kept herself under control. "They wanted a link to the Company, and they used my father to get it."

Carter nodded. "That's the way I figure it. My guess is, Josh's employment record will surface in the next day or so. It will probably be rigged to show that he never left the Company at all. Hell, if any one of their own people had bought the farm in the course of the kidnapping, they would probably also be connected with some government agency."

"So the Russians have nothing to do with it?"

"I don't think Comrex ever planned to implicate the Russians. Let me put it this way: in Aldami's country right now, there is a soft socialist government that caters to both sides. Aldami gets kidnapped and it's blamed on the CIA. That puts the current government on the spot. They have Marxist rebels in their backyard screaming for them to sever relations with America. They supposedly have the Soviets building sub bases."

Now she was getting it. "Comrex steps in, rescues Aldami in the nick of time, and moves in to settle the Madagascar government's problem."

Carter nodded. "Just like Grenada, only they don't leave."

"But how can they stay?"

"That," Carter said, "is still a mystery. But I intend to find out. Godiva is back. Let's go."

They got to the beach just as Godiva was getting into the skiff. The two women pushed off and Carter manned the oars. Minutes later they were in the cabin belowdecks around a small table.

"How did it go?"

"I made the call," Godiva replied, shaking her head as if she still didn't understand it all. "The woman seemed wary until I spoke all that gobbledygook, then she opened up."

The "gobbledygook" was a nonsense code that, when used properly, told Ginger Bateman that her field agent was too hot to make contact and that the present caller could be trusted. Carter had used it more than once before in tight spots.

"You gave her my version of what went down here?"

"I did. She took the number and called me back in an hour."

"And . . . ?" Carter asked.

"Your people think they have a working knowledge of Comrex. She says she can give it all to you in person three days from now, in Rio. She also said you're hotter than a firecracker. You'll have to get to Rio on your own."

Carter turned to Parks. "Got any ideas?"

The other man thought for a moment, then nodded. "Maybe."

"Same day rate," Carter said, "in advance."

"This one's on the house," the ex-boxer told him, and spread a map on the table. "I can land you in Costa Rica, here, in Puntarenas. Can you fly?"

"Anything but a jumbo jet," Carter replied.

"Guy by the name of Sego runs a freight ferry service. He sets up a run, you take it, one of his boys brings the plane back."

Carter studied the map. "Okay, have him set the run up to Caracas. With new papers, I can go commercial out of there to Rio."

"I think Sego can set you up with papers," Parks said with a smile. "He's been known to move a few people around."

Trilby leaned forward, placing her palms flat on the map. "Make those papers for two."

Carter was about to object, but seeing the set of her jaw, he paused. "You sure?"

"I'm sure."

"It's against my better judgment, but you might come in handy. Godiva, go back into the village. Make the call the same way, and tell them it's a go. Also, in Rio I'll need fresh papers, real ones, for Trilby and myself."

"Got it," the big woman replied.

"Thanks. And while you're there, hit a drugstore. Get whatever you need to turn Trilby into a brunette and me into a blond."

Godiva nodded and was gone. Rocco Parks headed forward to get on the radio to his friend in Costa Rica.

Trilby slumped back in her chair. "In for a penny, in for a pound."

"Yeah," Carter said. "Let's hope that's all we're in for."

Wynne paused in his stroll forward and leaned over to speak to the Learjet's only other passenger. "Comfortable?"

Bevello Aldami stirred the drink on the tray in front of him and looked up under heavily hooded eyes. "As comfortable as one can be under the circumstances."

Wynne smiled. "If you would like to nap, just call the steward. He'll make up the bed for you in the rear compartment."

The pilot's voice came over the bulkhead speaker

above the two men. "Mr. Wynne, your call has been patched through."

"Excuse me," Wynne said, and moved forward through the galley to a small conference booth just behind the cockpit. "General?"

"Yes, my boy, congratulations! From the news reports, everything went well?"

"Yes, sir. None of our people was injured. There was a hitch . . ."

"You missed Royce's daughter and the agent, Carter."

"We did, sir. I left Isabel and Cruz behind. Hopefully, they will pick up the trail."

"Yes," the general replied, "let us hope that they do. I've instructed our people in Washington to keep up the pressure."

"I am assuming that Carter will be told to go undercover and stay there by his people. Cruz should be able to get a scent when he moves. The Mexican police are cooperating fully with us."

"Good. What is your ETA to Lisbon?"

"Just about four hours, sir. What's the situation on Aldami's home turf?"

"Chaos, my boy, chaos! It's perfect! We should be able to walk in and take over in a week's time. How is your passenger?"

"Comfortable."

"See that he stays that way, Wynne. Keep him happy, very happy."

"Yes, sir."

FOURTEEN

From the high terrace, Carter squinted against the glare of the sun making its diamonds on the emerald bay, and sampled the sangria. The wine was harsh, as it should be to offset the sweetening effect of the fruits, the bananas and overripe apples, the wedges of pink grapefruit and orange. Good sangria has globules of fire lurking among the hidden ice cubes. It is a heady drink, one to do things to the blood, but, out of deference to the climate, should be consumed at a temperature low enough to frost the tonsils.

Beside him, Trilby lounged on a chaise in a string bikini. For a moment he let the appeal of her lush curves push the doubts of what lay ahead from his mind.

Remarkable, the changes that had taken place between little girl and grown woman.

He remembered the gangly, awkward, undeveloped girl. She had always been precocious and friendly. Every time he had visited Josh, she had attached herself to him, not in any pestering way, but in an easy, comfortable manner. So often had he met her that on the rare occasions she wasn't around he had noticed her absence. She could be habit-forming, he thought, especially now that she was a woman. With her long thick hair cascading over her perfect shoulders, a slim waist, the firm bust, a mischievously arched mouth and those long legs, she was a remarkably beautiful young woman. It was as simple as that. Yet not so simple. Suddenly, he felt old.

"What are you thinking?" Her hair, now a glossy dark brown, lay across the side of her face. Through the soft waves he could see one eye open and squinting up at him.

"Lascivious thoughts," he admitted with a grin.

She made a face. "This is unreal."

"We'll have to take it as it comes. We're the guests of a wealthy import-export trader named Sego until he can get us out of here."

"Do you think we can trust him? He looks shifty to me."

"If he wasn't shifty he couldn't pull this off. That's why he can be trusted. Besides, he likes the Yankee dollar, and I gave him a lot of them."

He poured more sangria into his glass and pulled his eyes from Trilby's body.

They had arrived five hours earlier, around noon. To Carter's surprise, Rocco Parks had pulled the *California Dreamin'* brazenly into Puntarenas harbor and tied up at a private pier next to a floating palace.

The yacht and the pier, Parks had explained, both belonged to Sego. Evidently the customs people also belonged to Sego, because no agents appeared to check papers or cargo.

The boat was scarcely secured when a Mercedes limousine glided onto the pier and a man stepped from its rear door. The long, aquiline face with its short, pointed beard, the smooth, olive-brown skin, could only have belonged to a Spaniard.

As Sego stepped aboard, Carter noticed that the pupils of his eyes never moved and his mouth had a cruel yet sensual quality.

He embraced Parks and Godiva, and turned to Carter. "I do not wish to know your names nor why you are in need of my services. I understand you are an accomplished pilot."

"I am," Carter replied.

"The plane is a Cherokee twin two-forty."

"I'm familiar with it."

"Good. You will come with me, please."

The good-byes and thank-yous to Rocco Parks and his lady were brief. In the limousine, behind dark windows, Sego spoke in clipped, rapid-fire sentences in barely accented English.

"I have a villa on the bluffs about four miles north of the city. I am currently staying in my town house, so the villa will be at your disposal."

"And how long will that be?" Carter asked.

"Hopefully, no more than a day. My driver's name is Rafael. Once I leave you in the city, Rafael will take you on to the villa. I will not see or contact you again. Rafael will be your only contact. Is that understood?"

Carter nodded.

The car halted in front of an imposing three-story house in a tree-shaded street. Sego prepared to get out.

"As I told you, I do not know who you are and I do not want to know. But I have many ears, and in this country, because of our neighbors' troubles, there are many representatives of the U.S. government. My ears tell me that the American agents here have received orders to watch for a man and woman. I would suggest that once you reach the villa, you do not leave it.''

Then he was gone and the limousine was speeding up the coastal highway.

The house was huge, old, and exquisitely proportioned, with its front windows and pillared portico looking down on the sea.

Rafael ushered them inside and wasted no time explaining where everything was. As he spoke, he set up a camera on a tripod.

''Sit. Passport photos.''

They sat and he snapped. As soon as he had their complete sizes, down to Trilby's bra, he put the camera under his arm and left.

''Are you hungry?''

''What?'' Carter said, jerking his mind back to the present.

''I asked if you were hungry. I checked the larder and it's loaded. How about a steak for an early dinner?''

''Great.''

''I'll shower and change.''

She moved away into the house and Carter saw the limo pull into the drive. Rafael got out and lugged two good-sized suitcases into the villa. Carter met him in the vast living room.

He dropped the bags and pointed to each in turn. ''New clothes, you, her.'' He fumbled in his jacket and came out with two thick envelopes. ''Papers for you. Passport, driving license, pilot license, and birth certificate. Same for lady except for pilot papers.''

Carter slit open the envelopes and looked them over. He was Nolan Cartwright, a British subject. Trilby was Teresa Carbone, American. Her occupation was listed as systems analyst. They were both listed as employees of SouthAm Freight and Ferry. Carter supposed this was one of Sego's companies.

"Papers real. Just your photos phony. You understand?"

"I understand," Carter replied.

"Good job. Your flight plan okay tomorrow morning. I pick you up at seven. Goo-bye."

And he was gone.

Carter hefted the bags and walked down the corridor to Trilby's bedroom. Without thinking he nudged the door open with his hip and walked in. "Oops, sorry . . ."

She was bent over at the edge of the bed patting her legs dry. She was nude, and the little bit the string bikini had covered was as good as the parts it hadn't.

She looked up at him and let the towel slide from her hands. Their eyes locked and suddenly she smiled. "Don't be."

Carter coughed and hoisted one of the bags to the bed. "The service around here is great. According to the driver, we have complete new wardrobes."

She had moved to his side and the scent of her freshly soaped body filled his nostrils.

"Nick . . ." He turned. "Does it bother you that I'm all grown up now?"

"Frankly, yes."

She moved forward until the tips of her jutting breasts touched his chest. Her hands on her hips, she raised her shoulders in an upward-stretching movement, her face showing that she was luxuriating in the touch of breast rubbing against breast. Her face also reflected her pleasure in his reaction to a confrontation with unabashed lust. His expression revealed nothing more than calm appreciation.

He made no move to shed his own clothing. The unspoken rules of the game called for his awaiting her move. She was his hostess in this room. The feast was hers to serve.

Moving into him, she placed her hands on his chest, pushing him gently to a seated position on the bed. She knelt before him at his feet. Carter had been undressed by women before, but he couldn't recall having experienced the degree of sensuousness with which this young woman loosened the strings on his trunks and tugged them down over his legs.

Her lips were moist as she spread his legs and, rising, moved between them until her breasts touched his face. Slowly she lowered herself, her hands inspecting the muscled expanse of his chest and shoulders. Her eyes remained fixed on his, her wet lips parted only slightly, revealing bright white teeth, and communicating an animal desire that a civilized refinement of the ancient rites was holding in check.

It was with a sense of ceremony that her fingers caressed his thighs and moved slowly upward.

"You've got marvelous patience," she said in a husky voice.

"I'm told it's a virtue," Carter said.

Kneeling again between his legs, she looked into his face with a mock demureness. "In that case, let's see just how virtuous you can be."

With a violent turn of her head, her long dark hair whirled around in front of her face. When the movement was completed, Carter saw that a good strand of it was now dangling from between her teeth. The impish gleam in her eyes told him what was coming next. It was an effort, but he forced his facial muscles into a patient smile.

He could not, however, stop the shudder that traveled from the root of him throughout his body, when, as her devilish eyes laughed into his, she lowered her face so as to allow the featherlike ends of her teeth-clenched hair to brush lightly against him as her hands formed a sheath and her fingertips were transformed into a thousand delights.

There was no analogy to what he felt, the sensations caused by those tiny touches. They were soft bites of a thousand benevloent insects; they were clean and pleasurable slices of a thousand minuscule knives whose blades alternated from sun-hot to iceberg-cold.

Again his body shuddered violently. He felt the welling up of restrained power deep within him, knew he couldn't take much more of this. And her eyes, now smiling at him, told him she also knew. Still, however, the movements of the hands continued, somehow impossibly building up her finger and palm rhythm to greater speed and pressure. When her teeth parted to let the hair fall from her mouth, there was no doubt what the next and final phase of her treatment would be.

A hammering, blood-pulsing spasm was Carter's response, followed by another. The third time, he exploded.

After she had pushed him gently back onto the bedspread, she crawled up and joined him, molding the long length of her body to his.

"Dinner now?" she cooed in his ear while her hands still moved over his body.

"No."

"Oh?'

"Now it's your turn."

She hesitated as he reached around her waist and drew her close. Her belly curved invitingly. He kissed it and felt her tremble. He kissed lower and, after a moment, there was a slight parting of her thighs, enough to allow his tongue to explore.

She was sweet there, sweet and warm and fragrant. Her mound trembled against his lips and he heard her breathing quicken. Her hands closed on his head and her fingers stroked through his hair. And then she drew back, whispering, "Now . . . please!"

Her legs wound about his hips and he entered her. Instantly their bodies set up a matching rhythm. In no time she began to gasp and threw her head from side to side. Then she locked her ankles at his back, thrust her hips high, and cried aloud with the joy of release.

But Carter didn't stop. He slowed and started back up the mountain again.

Her face found the crevice between his neck and shoulder, settling there. Her hands met in the small of his back, clasping together, then loosening, as her dagger-tipped fingers, velvet claws, probed the straining cords of his flesh. He was engulfed in her wondrous feminine depths. Her legs were vises, protective and imprisoning, as she conveyed him on the rolling crest of her desire.

Carter jerked away, bolting upright in bed. Disoriented for a moment, he glanced around the room, then at the woman in bed beside him.

Trilby.

Her now-dark hair fanned out on the pillow. Beneath the sheet that covered her, the lines of her legs and the roll of her breasts were soft. Her look seemed peaceful.

She moaned, then turned over, pulling the sheet up over her shoulders, exposing her back and the top of her buttocks. Standing, Carter reached over and tugged the sheet down over her back, then started around the bed to the bathroom.

She rustled. "What're you doing?" she asked without moving or opening her eyes.

"Covering you up and going to the head," he answered.

"Okay," she murmured, and fell asleep again.

He went on into the bathroom. He took a long shower, scrubbed himself dry with a white scratchy towel, then came back out.

Trilby was sitting up in the bed rubbing the sleep from her eyes. "What time is it?"

"A little after six. Shake a leg, we've got a plane to catch."

"You know what?"

"What?"

"We never did get around to that steak."

Carter grinned. "There are many kinds of nourishment."

FIFTEEN

The flight to Caracas was uneventful. The Cherokee was a dream to fly, and with the assistance of a stiff tail wind, they made excellent time. By the time Carter checked them through customs, they had nearly two hours before the Varig flight to Rio.

Trilby had a questioning look on her face when Carter grabbed the bags and headed toward the terminal exit.

"What the hell is going on?"

He grinned. "We're going to take a little tour of Caracas."

They took a cab into the city. At the office of a travel agent, Carter instructed the driver to stop and wait.

Inside, he bought tickets on the Varig flight to Rio and got boarding passes. Back in the cab, he told the driver he wanted to see the city, all of it.

They arrived at the airport exactly twenty minutes before boarding, and checked their bags with a porter outside the terminal doors.

Inside, Carter gently shoved Trilby forward with a hand in the small of her back. "You go first. We're not flying together."

She moved across the concourse. Carter darted into a nearby gift shop, snatched up a magazine, and, over it, searched the area.

Trilby moved into the line behind a pale, long-haired girl in faded jeans, sweatshirt, and fringed leather jacket.

Seated as if he were waiting for the line to move faster was a tall, lanky man. A floppy hat shadowed his eyes, and a scruffy beard and ragged sideburns hid the rest of his face.

Carter nixed Floppy Hat and kept looking.

It didn't take long to spot him: medium size with long arms and whitish hands and long fingers. His suit was brown, good material and well tailored. His trousers were pressed knife-sharp and the cuffs barely touched the tops of what appeared to be cowboy boots with high heels. Actually they were low shoes with cowboy heels. His face was gaunt. His eyes, darting first to his palm, then up at Trilby, then back down to his palm again, were urgent and contained.

When he got that look on his face and started to move, Carter moved with him.

After about a hundred feet, the man darted off the main concourse into a narrow hallway. Above the entrance were the international symbols for telephones and rest rooms.

He was just pumping coins into the phone when Carter jammed a finger into his back.

"Let's go into the john and talk, friend."

The man moved. Just inside the door, Carter grabbed his belt and yanked hard. The man squealed in pain as his balls were forced up into his belly, but he was no quitter.

He twisted out of Carter's grasp, whirled, and bucked

into the Killmaster like a rodeo bull. Carter slammed into the door, and the other man came up, cat-fast, with a blade, aiming to kill. Sheer instinct made Carter duck as the blade flailed at his head.

The wild swing carried him halfway around and threw him off-balance. Carter rushed in, slamming at the hard-muscled belly with a left. He went down snarling, losing the knife, but he grabbed Carter's ankle and he tripped, falling headlong past him, belly-flopping on his face.

He lost his grip on Carter's ankle. The Killmaster yanked free and got up winded, turning to face him. The man was getting to his feet slowly, hands low and slightly forward, faking a daze.

He drove at Carter again, throwing a left, but Carter blocked it and hooked his own left at the side of his jaw. The head jerked back, and Carter used the edge of his hand against his stretched neck. You can kill a man that way, by breaking his trachea.

The wheezing in his throat told how spent he was. Carter was gasping for breath too. He pounded at his belly and chest until it was torture every time Carter sucked air into his own lungs.

He wouldn't quit, falling back against the wall, letting it bounce him at Carter, lashing with clublike blows. Carter could feel his eye closing, his nose dripping blood. The right side of his mouth was numb.

Carter got him away from the wall. Suddenly he lurched forward in a diving, rolling tackle that brought Carter down. They rolled over and over, using knees and elbows. The man cursed. He bit Carter's hand. The Killmaster pulled it away. The man tried for Carter's good eye, his thumb stabbing down like a spike, missing by an inch, raking the cheekbone. Carter jammed his knee into the other man's groin and he cried out in agony, relaxing his grip for an instant. Carter fell away and managed to stand.

The man got to his hands and knees. Carter staggered closer, his good eye staring at his unprotected face, the easiest target ever for Carter's boot. But Carter's knees felt boneless.

The Killmaster found his voice. "You're mean, cowboy, but I'm meaner."

The other man managed a smile. "Mean, shit, pardner, you're dead."

Carter took a wild right on his left shoulder, which opened the man up. The blade of the Killmaster's fingers found the other man's windpipe.

It wasn't enough to kill. The kill came as he was falling. Carter got the back of his head and his chin in his hands and let the man's own weight break his neck as he fell.

Carter dragged him into a stall and propped him up with his pants around his ankles. He stripped the pockets, locked the door, and crawled over the top of it.

At one of the basins, he repaired his face as much as he could and covered the rest of it with dark glasses.

Back on the concourse hurrying toward the gate, he thumbed through the ID. The man was Chad Harris, GS-10, field agent, CIA. There was nothing in the papers to even hint at what his current official assignment was, or even if he was on assignment at all. The other item of interest Carter found was a snapshot, head and shoulders, of Trilby. It was just about the right size to fit in the man's palm.

The Killmaster pocketed the photograph. He could guess its source, but he would question her about it.

As he dropped the wallet and credentials case down a

trash recepticle, Carter hoped that Chad Harris had been one of Aldami's abductors.

He barely made it through the gate before they battened up and removed the jetway.

As he passed Trilby's seat, she mouthed, "Trouble?"

He shook his head slightly and hoped his lip hadn't started to bleed again.

In his seat, four rows behind Trilby, Carter scribbled a note and carefully folded it. He would drop it in her lap on his way to the john as soon as they were airborne.

It was a good supposition that if they had a man in Caracas hotfooting it from gate to gate as a spotter, they would have at least two or more in Rio.

The Killmaster was pretty sure by now that the Comrex people didn't have a positive ID on him. And even with a general one, the blond hair and mustache would throw them off.

Trilby, with only sunglasses and a dye job on her hair, was a different story.

After several hundred thousand miles of flying, Carter knew airline personnel routine like the back of his hand. A flight attendant's uniform usually consisted of scarf, blouse, jacket, skirt, and slacks. If she wears the slacks on the outbound leg, she will wear the skirt on the inbound leg.

The note Carter passed to Trilby was in a cryptic shorthand, but she was a bright lady and he was sure she would pick up on it.

About a half hour before landing, he stood and moved forward to the galley. It was a relaxed time for the attendants. Most of them had congregated in the midship galley, chatting.

He appeared a littly tipsy, but the attendant he had

zeroed in on agreed to pour him just one more drink. He promptly spilled it on her slacks as if by accident.

He apologized all over the place and returned to his seat, nodding at Trilby as he passed.

The stewardess reached into her airline-issue suitcase and hit one of the rest rooms with a skirt in her hands. Minutes later she emerged and hung the stained slacks alongside her uniform jacket in the storage area used for hanging carry-on luggage.

Trilby leaned into the aisle, and Carter nodded.

Up and away he went again. This time his bulk filled one end of the galley across from where the target slacks and jacket hung.

Again he apologized profusely, offered to pay for the cleaning, and generally went on and on. He sensed rather than saw Trilby pass behind him and dart into the lavatory. When the attendant assured him that everything was fine, he returned to his seat.

They were on final approach when Trilby emerged and took her seat with a nod to Carter. The slacks rolled up under her full skirt didn't bulge. She carried a good-sized purse, and it did bulge with the attendant's jacket.

As the plane taxied to the gate, there was a lot of chatter around the galley, mainly about the missing uniform jacket, but Carter knew they would never dream of accusing a passenger of stealing it.

Trilby managed to be at the door when it opened. Carter hung back, keeping her in sight. She darted into the first rest room just inside the terminal, and in two minutes emerged in the uniform. The blouse was blue instead of white and she had no scarf, but Carter was betting that they wouldn't notice.

He was right.

There were two of them: a woman at the end of the

customs line, and a man just beyond to pick up the tail. They were both checking passengers against palms, just as the cowboy in Caracas had done.

Trilby breezed past them without a glance: the uniform made her almost invisible.

Now it was Carter's turn, and he drew no more interest. Two escalators took him to the baggage claim area.

AXE's local Rio man was Luis Escobar, a plump, dark-skinned Portuguese-Brazilian in a sweatshirt, baggy trousers, and jogging shoes. Carter was on top of him before the other man saw the light.

"Luis, how are you?"

"Fine, fine, you've gotten younger," he replied dryly. "How was the flight?"

"Excellent," Carter said, leaning forward and lowering his voice. "Which car is yours?"

"Red Volkswagen, down there, end of the line. A little beat-up."

"Get the bags," Carter said, pressing the claim checks into the other man's hand and moving through the exit doors into the bright sunshine.

Far to his right he could see Trilby stepping into a taxi. He turned left toward the car. It was unlocked. By the time Carter had settled in, Escobar was waddling up with the bags. He tossed them into the back seat and oozed behind the wheel.

"The woman?"

"Taxi. They'll be parked near the Stradi at Copacabana."

"Good, it's on the way. Hang on."

The Volkswagen coughed, spit, sputtered, and lurched from the curb. Carter settled back, lit a cigarette, and let his mind go blank.

The sun was hot and bright, and Sugar Loaf Mountain

rose up out of the bright blue water against a bright blue sky, gray and green and topped by the little white restaurant in its garden of hibiscus and pines. One of the orange cable cars was creaking its way up there, a thousand feet above the red tile rooftops, as they drove along the wide tree-lined sweep of the Flamenco.

Luis Escobar drove like a madman in his locally assembled Volkswagen, taking shortcuts against the traffic in one-way streets and once overtaking a long line of cars by driving along the sidewalk. A policeman yelled at him, but Escobar took no notice except to yell back a vigorous insult and run the red light. He saw the look on Carter's face and shrugged. "Everybody does it, why should we have to wait, it's a free country."

The beach at Copacabana was crowded, and kids were flying brightly colored paper kites and playing soccer on the hot sand. Carter saw a mailman there, stripped down to his shorts and lying asleep with his head on his mail sack. If he slept for too long, or got carried away by the warmth of the sun and the sound of the surf, he'd dump his mail when no one was looking and report back with his empty sack. Another day, another cruzeiro. . . .

"There, Luis," Carter said, pointing.

Escobar made a U-turn in front of four oncoming cars and slid in behind the taxi. Trilby spotted them. She shoved some bills in the driver's hand and ran back to the Volkswagen.

"How did we do?" she asked, folding into the back seat between the two bags.

"Good," Carter said, and smiled. "We're still alive. Luis Escobar, Trilby Royce."

"Hello."

Escobar grabbed her hand and kissed it savagely. "Ah,

you are beautiful, truly beautiful! Say you would like to make babies with a fat Brazilian roué!"

Carter roared with laughter. "Fly us out of here, Luis. Don't pay any attention to him, Trilby. He has two wives and ten kids already."

The hotel La Martinique was right at the upper end of Ipanema. It was a white, ten-story sawtoothed affair with tiny triangular terraces that gave the illusion of privacy for all the outside rooms. The lobby had raw air conditioning, unctuous hospitality, goose bumps on naked shoulders, and slashes of color, as if a Latin-American architect had had illicit relations with Danish modern.

Escobar had jammed the car into a space too small for even a Volkswagen. Grabbing the bags, he had led them into the lobby and directly toward the elevators.

"You are already registered. I'll give them the names on the passports later. I got just one suite." He winked and Trilby got a little rosy in the cheeks.

There was constant movement out on an acre of sun chaises lining the beach, around the free-form swimming pool and outdoor bar. Traffic via lobby to grill and elevators had the Miami look: women with poodles and black glasses; deeply tanned playboys; older wolves in youthful casuals on the prowl for either sex; and the kind of lovelies who wouldn't think twice about trying to clip the Johns for whatever the traffic would bear.

The suite was on the top floor and it was cleverly disguised as posh. Escobar dropped the bags and pointed out the bath to Trilby.

"I would adore scrubbing your back," he leered.

Trilby just shook her head and walked into the bedroom, closing the door behind her. Escobar instantly became all business, grabbing the phone, dialing, and handing it to Carter.

"Yes?"

"It's me, we're in."

"Want me to come there?" Ginger Bateman asked.

"Have you got some scotch there?"

"Of course."

"I'll come there."

"Suite Nine-oh-one, right below you."

Carter hung up. Escobar stretched out on the couch with a 9mm Beretta across his belly.

"I will make sure the young lady doesn't have any visitors while you are gone," he announced cheerfully.

Carter took the stairs and rapped twice on the door of 901. It opened immediately, and he was barely inside when a glass was shoved into his hand.

"Chivas, three fingers, one cube. Glad you made it, Nick, since you so royally fucked up in Puerto Vallarta. Let's sit by the windows."

Carter followed her with his feet and eyes, sipping the drink. She wore a peasant blouse and skirt that couldn't hide a figure to end all figures. Her thick sable hair bounced about her shoulders and the look on her face was stern.

For this go-round, Ginger Bateman was all business, and Carter went along with it.

The table in front of the long windows overlooking the beach was piled with computer printouts.

"It took a lot of digging and matching, but the people in Research did one hell of a job. On the names you gave us we went clear back to diapers. Nothing in their lives was missed."

Carter watched her arrange index cards until they resembled teams in a sports tournament.

"The working relationship, social connections, and war records read like this." She rattled off the names of Kirby, D'Ambrosio, Josh Royce, Wynne, Cruz, and a dozen others. As she did this, she rearranged the cards. When she finished, the cards belonging to Cal Wynne and Brigadier General Jeffrey Cornwall were at the center.

"Then those two are the top dogs?" Carter asked.

"We thought so at first," Ginger said. "But after we finished with the names, we fed in dates, places, and, most importantly, results. By results I mean the end result of some known Comrex operation. None of these people qualified with the clout nor the access to delicate and oftentimes supersecret information that would have to be known for such successful results. Am I getting too involved?"

Carter smiled and nodded. "Really, you are. Why not just tell me who I've got to kill and why?"

The look was smoldering. Bateman, like her boss David Hawk, liked to couch AXE's job in euphemisms. Nevertheless, she turned over a final card and placed it in the center of the maze where the final game of the tournament would be.

Carter narrowed his eyes and felt a chill quiver up his spine as he spoke the name out loud. "Major General Adrian Dillon. Isn't that a little farfetched?"

Bateman shook her head. "Part of what we found is fact, some of it supposition. But Research thinks it's damn good supposition."

Carter blinked and conjured up the image of the old warhorse, Adrian Dillon.

He was a self-made military man who'd bucked the leftists and the liberals all his life. As a young captain in Korea under MacArthur, Dillon had gotten himself in hot water more than once by declaring that MacArthur was right and Truman was wrong: American forces should cross the 38th Parallel and blow the Reds to hell.

The older he got, the farther right he had moved. He scared a lot of people, but he had also gained a lot of respect. He had served all over the world as an advisor and/or covert operations officer for the National Security Council and the CIA. By the time he'd reached his top job as chief procurement officer at the Pentagon, he was one of the most hated *and* loved men in the country.

Carter said so, and Bateman chimed in. "He was also one of the most feared, Nick. By the time he had been retired two years, he had made wealthy friends who believed the same way he did, and were willing to put their money behind their beliefs. We can't prove it, but we also think that those he *didn't* make friends with, he blackmailed."

"My God . . . defense contractors, suppliers, corporate officers whose jobs depended on goverment contracts . . ."

"Exactly. Dillon fits the picture to the last dot. Most of these people at the top of the Comrex power structure were intimate associates of Dillon's at one time or another. And there's another fact, Nick, that's not too widely known. The general is an expert on African politics and military affairs."

Here she paused and upended a thick briefcase over the table. Two thick manuscripts bound with rubber bands tumbled out.

"We got wind of these by pure luck. They were too radical to be published, but the agent in New York who tried to peddle them at the time remembered that he had copies in his files. Check 'em out—I'll pour you three more fingers and make one for myself."

She moved across the room and Carter took the rubber bands from the heavy manuscripts. One was titled ''The Americanization of Africa''; the other was ''Africa: Red, Dead, Or Free.''

He scarcely noticed Ginger's return to the table. At the end of an hour he grabbed the glass, sat back, and sighed loudly.

''Dillon's *Mein Kampf* in two volumes.''

She nodded. ''It would appear so. Ten years ago he tried to tell the world what he was going to do, and no one paid any attention.''

''Now he's doing it, and no one can do anything about it. What does Hawk think?''

''The situation is terrible in Madagascar, and getting worse. The Pentagon is putting pressure on the president to do something about it, even covertly. We think that's coming from Dillon's cronies.''

Carter rose and began to pace. ''But officially we can't do anything, so under the table a private group has offered to ransom Aldami and go into the country and suppress the rebels.''

Bateman nodded. ''Comrex has never been mentioned, but we don't think there is any doubt.''

''I still don't understand one thing,'' Carter said. ''Even if Comrex moves into the country, how in God's name could they get any power and keep it?''

''Hawk thinks it's Aldami. Comrex moves, puts Aldami in power, then, against his will, rules with him as a figurehead. We've managed to intercept some of their communictions. A constant in all of them is the name Madras.''

''Madras?''

''Yes. The connotation is Madras as the power, Madras as a play on words for money . . . Madras-Midas. It's a constant. Hawk thinks Madras is a code name for Bevello Aldami.''

Carter stopped and slid back into his chair. ''Then they key is Aldami.''

''If we get him back, Nick, we can stop them. They won't have any ace to play.''

''All we have to do is find him.''

''We think we've got that, too. Early yesterday morning, General Dillon and three of his aides left for a fishing trip in Maine. They got there, but they didn't stay. A Lear belonging to Benzinger Enterprises left Bangor airport an hour after the general's arrival. There were four passengers. The pilot of the Lear filed a flight plan for Lisbon.''

''Can you be sure?''

''Nick, Harold Benzinger is General Dillon's son-in-law.''

''Castillo Augustine,'' Carter whispered.

Bateman nodded. ''We think it's their base of operations. I've already got people digging over there.''

''Getting into Portugal will be the biggest problem.''

Bateman smiled for the first time since he had entered the room. ''We've already got that figured as well.''

SIXTEEN

He called himself Smilin' Jack, and he even looked like the comic-strip character. He had been flying for years, and he just loved doing favors for important people who could one day do him a few favors in return.

It took twelve hours to ready the shipment and get the two special crates ready for transport.

Luis Escobar drove the truck himself that transported the crates to the airport. They were marked FRAGILE and ARTWORK.

Twenty minutes after takeoff, the sides were removed and there he was.

"Hi, there, y'all! I'm Smilin' Jack. Anything y'all want, lemme know. You can move around anywhere on the plane. They's coffee and sandwiches forward. I'll have you at Mariba, outside Seville, in nine hours flat!"

It was eight hours and forty minutes. In nine hours the two crates were tied securely on a flatbed truck and headed for the downtown area of Seville, where they were unloaded in a warehouse near the Maestranza bull-ring.

A half hour after their arrival, there was a light tapping

on the crate and the side was removed again. Carter crawled out and shook hands with Manuel Diaz, AXE Madrid.

"Carter, you never cease to amaze," the man said, shaking his head. "Who's in the other one?"

"The belle of the ball."

Together they unfastened the side of Trilby's crate and she crawled out. "Never again—it's like being buried alive," she groaned. "Who are you?"

"Manuel Diaz at your service, señorita. This way, please."

Carter grabbed the single bag they had brought along, and followed him.

In another corner of the warehouse was a little gray Datsun. Diaz wasted no time lifting the trunk lid. Inside was an Ingram machine pistol, some spare clips, a belt of grenades, and a paper bag. From the bag he withdrew three small pink cardboard boxes with cellophane windows.

"If you don't think this took some doing in this amount of time," he groused, pulling a brassiere from one of the boxes and holding it up for their inspection. "The underneath and side stays have been removed. The plastique has been molded in the shape of the stays, and resewn into all three bras."

Trilby felt the result. "Nobody wears these anymore. They cut you in half."

Carter took all three bras and put them in the bag. "Let's hope the general and his boys aren't up on ladies' lingerie."

"It's a continuous fuse with a detonator wire running through the center," Diaz continued. "You can snip it anywhere."

"And the transmitter?" Carter asked.

Diaz made a face and withdrew two small plastic boxes from his pocket. He opened one of them. "You're not going to like this. Suppositories."

Carter looked at Trilby. She stifled a giggle. "Okay, the map."

Diaz spread a map of Spain and Portugal on the hood of the car. "Go north to here. I've outlined the back roads. The best place to cross into Portugal is here. From about here they'll probably pick you up."

"The plan's been passed around?"

Diaz nodded. "Secret cables from Paris to Madrid to Washington and back again. If they have the kind of intelligence you think they have, they'll know you're coming."

"I don't get it," Trilby said. "If we want them to know we're coming, why didn't we just fly commercial into Lisbon?"

"Because," Carter replied, "we want to look like we're real sneaky and smart."

"Here's the last thing on your list," Diaz said, "The floor plan of the *castillo*. Good hunting."

He crossed to the big double doors and started tugging them open.

In the car, Carter started the engine and dropped the floor plan on Trilby's lap.

"Start memorizing that."

"Nick . . ."

"Yeah?"

"What if they make me take all my clothes off and we can't get to the suitcase?"

Carter gave her a mock shudder. "Don't even think of such things."

He dropped the clutch and the powerful little Datsun roared toward the sunlight.

• • •

The road that Diaz had marked northward out of the city was little more than a goat path. The farther they went, the worse it seemed to get. By noon they had wound their way around half a dozen Moorish-style castles and passed through as many blistering sun-steeped villages. In one of these, Carter stopped for fuel beside a rusty pump that must have been there before Franco.

He found a few trees behind the station and relieved himself. Inside, he bought two sodas and paid for the gas.

Trilby was leaning against the front of the car when he handed her a bottle. She took it absently.

"Something wrong?" he asked.

"Yeah. Do you really think we can pull this off?"

"Darlin', let's get something straight. You may think I'm a bit nuts, and I probably am, but believe me, I have no death wish. Yeah, I think we can pull this off. If I didn't, we wouldn't be here. Get in!"

They took off, stirring dust in the sun-swollen air, winding through bare hills with distant snow-capped mountains sharp against the sky. Donkeys clogged the way, their saddlebags bulging with hay or wood. Now and then they passed wagons hooped with canvas, pulled by evil-smelling mules. Gypsies.

They arrived in a tiny village called Sierra Minas around three. The single, unpaved street was pitifully poor, occupied by scraggly chickens, dogs, and skinny kids in brightly colored rags who ran after the car begging for money.

"What do you think?" Carter asked.

"About what?"

"We stay the night here, or go on to Oliva de la Frontera. That's our jumping-off place across the frontier."

She looked up and down the two-block-long street. "Do you think there's a bathtub in town?"

"No."

She shuddered. "Let's go on."

With cart paths instead of roads it took them nearly three hours. Oliva de la Frontera was a decent-sized town and very Spanish. Houses with grillwork windows and doors lined most of the streets. Through them they could see cool courtyards paved in pink marble with walls tiled a deep blue, where oleanders, roses, and jasmine bloomed in jars around a center fountain.

"This is . . . romantic!" Trilby cried, and suddenly sobered. "Do you think they're watching us right now?"

"No. We only let them know we're coming, not how. I'd say they won't pick up on us until we're within fifty miles of Castillo Augustine. So Oliva can be . . ."

"What?"

"Romantic," he finished. "We'll start working on it as soon as we hit the hotel."

The hotel was old-world Spanish charm, and clean, with a cool, tiled lobby.

"Ah, señor and señora, you are welcomed to Oliva!"

He was a bull-necked, stocky, curly-haired young man with an engaging smile and an obvious desire to use what English he had. He looked like the stable boy, but happened to be, with his mother, the owner of the hotel.

Carter explained their needs in Spanish and signed the register.

While Trilby took a long bath, Carter checked out the town just in case they had to make a fast exit.

Back in the lobby, he explained that since they had to get an early start in the morning, would it be possible to break Spanish tradition and have dinner before ten o'clock?

"But of course, señor!" the enthusiastic young man proclaimed. "I will serve you and the señora myself!"

Trilby was still in the tub. Carter stripped and climbed in with her. By mutual consent all they did was soak.

True to his word, the young man showed up at seven pushing a rolling tray. His shirt was still open to the navel, but now it was clean and he had a rose behind his ear.

He put the rose in a small vase, opened the wine, kissed Trilby's hand, and left discreetly.

The dinner was delicious, and over it they eyed each other in the candlelight. When it was finished, Carter poured the last of the wine. Trilby excused herself and slipped from the room.

A few moments later, he heard the tap of her heels on the tile floor and she appeared in something long, black, and lacy. She posed in the doorway with most of her ample bosom tantalizingly exposed and the rose in her teeth.

"I theeenk you never make good your word, *querido mio*." She moved into his arms, tucking her dark hair under the angle of his jaw and flattening her breasts against his chest.

"My word?"

"Hold me, keeess me."

He did, and got the message. He slowly and lightly stroked the smooth contours of her back, from the moist warmth of her shoulders down to the swelling curve of her hips. Her hair smelled like summer grass and fresh air.

The black, lacy thing dropped to the floor and she was in his arms and on her way to the bedroom.

The rest was romance, of course.

SEVENTEEN

Breakfast was a quick cup of coffee and rolls. By six they were on the dusty road out of Oliva de la Frontera. It took nearly an hour to cover the thirty-eight miles to the Portuguese border.

A half hour later, Trilby turned in the seat, a quizzical expression on her face. "When do we get into Portugal?"

"We crossed the frontier a half hour ago," Carter replied. "There are no border stations in this area. The people, mostly gypsies, pass back and forth daily."

They hit a gravel road northward and Carter picked up speed. Fifty miles farther on, he turned east again onto another goat path road that ran along the Sorraia River.

From here on, the land was rolling hills and hardly changing landscape dotted with acre after acre of vineyards. Signs were nil, or often wrong when they could be found. Directions were taken by the tiny villages.

By Carter's reckoning, the village of Cristos was about ninety hard miles from Castillo Augustine. It was there that he stopped for gas and lunch.

The main street of the village was one block long, and

its major business was a wine shop with one entire side open to the street.

He pulled around to the side where he had spotted a lone pump. He had scarcely killed the engine when a young boy in shorts and worn sneakers attacked the gas cap.

"What now?" Trilby asked.

"We eat."

"In there?"

"In there," Carter said, and took her elbow.

An old Coca-Cola sign hung above the door by one hinge. Inside, worn tables and benches were scattered across the floor. The air was heavy with the smoke of black tobacco, charcoal, and the steam of frying fish.

An old gypsy woman came from the kitchen slowly, her pendulous breasts cascading over her apron. She had a cigar, rolling it like a pencil between her fingers. A necklace of coins and religious medals sank into the folds of the skin at her throat.

"Bom dia," she croaked, dragging deeply on the cigar.

"Bom dia," Carter replied. *"Caldo verde?"*

"*Sim*" she said, nodding.

"Good," Carter continued in Portuguese. "We'll have the *Caldo verde*, and an order of *bacalhau à brás*."

"Sim."

The woman shuffled away. Over her shoulder, Carter could see that the hood of the Datsun was up and the young boy was halfway into the engine.

"What's for lunch?" Trilby asked, trying to get the snarls out of her hair.

"Kale and sausage soup, then sort of a cod omelet."

"What?"

He grinned. "Local specialty. You'll love it."

She managed to get halfway through the plateful of

fried fish, eggs, and onions before she pushed it away and finished the meal with wine and bread heavily coated with fresh butter.

The boy moved through and darted into the kitchen. He spoke to the woman, but Carter couldn't hear. He did hear part of the woman's sharp reply.

". . . speak softly, the blond one knows the tongue."

Carter smiled to himself and finished his wine. He paid and they moved outside. The young boy lounged against a wall, intent on torturing a lizard with a stick.

"Oil, water, everything all right under the hood?" Carter asked in Portuguese.

"*Sim, senhor*. Everything is full."

I'll bet, Carter thought, and slid behind the wheel.

About a mile outside the village, the Killmaster swung off the road into a small grove of cork trees.

"Something wrong?"

He shook his head. "Depends on how you look at it. I think everything is going just fine."

He killed the engine and moved around to the trunk. Trilby stepped from the car and joined him.

"Are you doing what I think you're doing?"

He nodded. "Time to change your underwear." He paused. "And . . . the little plastic boxes Diaz gave us? Pick a tree."

She made a face.

He left her pulling her blouse over her head, and moved back to the front of the car. Under the hood he searched with a penlight until he found it: a directional beeper. It was magnetically attached to one of the struts securing the starter.

He left it where it was, closed the hood, and looked around. Trilby had found some bushes somewhere away from the car. He did the same.

She was already in the passenger seat when he got back in the car. "Everything all right?"

"Everything's fine. You?"

She did a little wriggle in the seat. "This stuff doesn't explode with perspiration, does it?"

He laughed and backed the Datsun out of the trees.

They stuck to the back roads, not pushing it. Beside him, Trilby was calm, almost napping. Carter drove with his eyes and ears alert to every sound or movement.

Oddly enough, she heard it first. "What was that?"

He dropped into neutral and let the engine idle. Then he heard it, a low droning sound in the distance.

He stopped the car and got out, his eyes searching the horizon. To the left of the road, a plain stretched away. To the right, the ground was also flat, but it ended in a thick gathering of steep hills, a part of those they'd just come through. He looked up the road to the ridge, and then back.

There was nothing there.

A slight wind threaded across the flats, trembling the trees. But there was nothing else. The sound was gone.

Then he heard it again. Faint. But there.

He turned toward the ridge.

"Oh, shit . . ." he growled, and jumped back into the car, backing it around. Then, jamming it into first, he gunned it off the road, speeding toward the cluster of hills about three miles away.

"What is it?" Trilby shouted over the screaming engine.

"Choppers," he answered. "Behind that ridge."

"You're sure?"

"That's the one sound I'll always know," he hissed,

while he pushed the gas pedal down more and careened around a tree. "Watch the ridge!" he ordered.

Trilby turned in the seat, and Carter brought the speed up. The steering wheel rattled hard in his hands, but he eased the car up to fifty, then sixty. The car felt as if it were coming apart between the potholes.

"Anything?" he asked.

"Not yet."

The hills slipped closer. He had the gas pedal to the floorboard. The speedometer said seventy.

"Jesus . . ." Trilby whispered.

They hammered through a sinkhole, vaulted airborne, and slammed back down, closing the shocks, plowing through dirt, but Carter held it, bringing it back straight.

In front of them, the hills were coming faster now, about two miles away. Carter could begin to make out details. A dry wash between two of the hills. He angled toward it.

"The ridge?"

"Still clear."

He swerved around a cork grove, skidded, then righted the car again. They crashed down a slight incline and drifted into another skid. Carter let off the gas.

He slowed a little more. Maneuvering around another bush, he came to the wash and turned along the top of it, following it toward the cleft it made in the hills.

"Nick . . . !" Trilby cried.

He snapped a look back toward the ridge, and saw them.

Two dark smears against the sky, dropping down the ridge and coming fast.

He looked back to the hills, less than a mile away.

The banks of the wash steepened and he eased down

into it, trying to keep to the sides and away from the middle and any pockets of sand.

"They must be doing a hundred miles an hour!" she gasped.

"They are," Carter muttered, and raked the car through a curve, dropping down the bank of the wash. Then he saw the log.

"Dammit!" He wrenched the wheel. The front tires missed the log, but the left rear caught it hard, smashing through the rotten wood, exploding, pivoting the Datsun around, nosing it down into the wash, slamming through a line of rock, then sinking the front tires down into the sandy middle.

Carter kicked his door open and looked back.

The helicopters were halfway between the ridge and the car.

"Under the car!" he shouted to Trilby as she climbed out her door.

They ran to the back of the car, and Carter crawled under it first. Trilby followed him. With the front of the car slanted into the sand, the space under it was small. Carter dug at it, hollowing a pocket for them.

"We should have tried for the hills," Trilby said, "to make it look good."

"This will do," Carter growled.

Then the frenzied pulse of the helicopter blades rushed down on them, hammering everything else away. Dirt and sand exploded in on them. Carter pulled the collar of his shirt up over his mouth and nose, and Trilby did the same with her windbreaker. The sand poured in on them, burying them, and Carter lost all sense of direction. The roar of the blades filled the wash, and he guessed they were circling, hovering.

More dirt blasted them, coming up over their heads. He fought for air, and next to him, he could feel Trilby screaming soundlessly. He pulled her to him, bringing his shirt up over her head.

"Did you expect this?" she yelled in his ear.

"Frankly, no. But it fits," he yelled back.

He chanced a look from under the car, shielding the sand from his eyes with a cupped hand.

It was a military maneuver. One chopper was landing. The other was going up about five hundred feet to hover When the first one settled and the engine muted down, the side door slid open.

Two men—one with a bull horn, the other with a submachine gun—appeared in the opening.

The bull horn blared. "Come out! If you are armed, throw the guns out first and come out from under the car!"

"What now?" Trilby asked, her body quivering against his.

"We make it look good."

"How do we do that?"

"We wait a little."

Suddenly the machine gun barked, stitching slugs along the side of the Datsun from the front bumper to the rear.

"You have five seconds! We will put the next burst underneath the car!"

"Now?" Trilby said.

"Now," Carter replied, and together they slithered from beneath the car and stood beside it, their hands away from the bodies.

The man with the bull horn jumped from the hatch and moved forward. The machine gunner and a third man, carrying an ugly sawed-off shotgun, dropped to the sand and flanked him as the three of them moved forward.

The one with the bull horn held a photograph beside Trilby's face and smiled. Then he turned to the Killmaster and his face became stone.

"First we talk, Carter, and then I show you what real retribution is. The men you killed were good soldiers."

Carter shrugged. "Most soldiers are good soldiers. It just depends what side they're on. I imagine you're Wynne."

The reply was a slap to the side of the head. It rocked Carter, but he went with it, softening the blow.

It was time to put the last scene in the charade.

Carter came in low and fast. He hit Wynne a one-two in the gut before the man realized he had even moved. The other two men were shocked into immobility.

But not for long.

Carter got another good one, right in the middle of Wynne's face. He felt and heard the nose give, and then all three of them were on him.

For a while he fought and held his own. When he judged it was time to give in, he let a blow land on the side of his head and went to the ground.

Then he let them go to work on him until blackness killed the pain.

Ginger Bateman was sure she had never been so tired in her life. She had been at it for nearly forty-eight hours with only a catnap since returning from Rio. She had been too tired to even drive, so she had taken a taxi from Dupont Circle to her apartment in Georgetown.

Now she didn't even bother to check her mail or messages. Removing her makeup was the last thought in her mind. The first thought was sleep.

She started discarding clothing at the front door and left a rumpled trail all the way into the bedroom.

Then, naked, she sprawled across the bed and buried her head between two pillows.

There was a dark tunnel that promised bliss and relief. She was halfway down it, when the phone brought her back.

"Yes, hello, what is . . . who . . . hello?"

"Ginger?"

"You've got the wrong number."

"Ginger, come to—"

"I don't want to."

"It's Steve Furman, Ginger, your trusty assistant still on the job."

She left the tunnel and struggled back to reality. "All right, Steve, what is it."

"Can you get right back down here? I think we've cracked Madras."

She rolled to a sitting position. "I'll be there in an hour."

With the promise of a twenty-dollar tip, the taxi driver made it in forty minutes.

Steve Furman, a computer genius and graduate of the CIA's top cryptography section, was waiting in her office with a fresh pot of coffee.

"All right, what have you got?" Ginger said, reaching for the pot and a cup.

"Plenty. We cracked the telex codes to six of the nine banks used by Comrex in Switzerland and the Cayman Islands. Here are the printouts."

Fortified by caffeine, Ginger went over the printouts, asked a few questions, and went over them again.

"My God," she said at last, "this means that Dillon

is just a cog . . . a big one, but just a cog in the big wheel.''

Furman nodded. ''Looks that way. That is, if we assume he who owns the purse strings is the *real* power in Comrex.''

Bateman rubbed her eyes and dropped into the chair behind her desk.

''Carter is in by now, and there's no way we can warn him.''

EIGHTEEN

Carter came awake feeling cold and clammy. He had the feeling of pushing his way through layer after layer of thick mist to a small, orange-colored light. When he finally opened his eyes, he found himself on his back staring at a timbered ceiling, his body bathed in sweat.

He lay still.

His wrists were held by rope, his arms pulled wide, bound down to the sides of a cot. The room was small and square. The cribwork walls were ironwood poles, pegged and mortised at the ends. The ceiling overhead was the same. When he turned his head he could see the door—ironwood posts set in timbers top and bottom. The door was unhinged, apparently lifted into place at considerable effort. It was a prison room.

And then it hit him. It was a dungeon room. More than likely, he was in the cellars of the Castillo Augustine.

The slot in the door opened. He saw an eye, heard a grunt, and the door itself opened wide.

There were three of them, all well dressed in suits. One of them stayed by the door holding a Beretta, the other two untied him.

"Can you walk?"

"Yes," Carter said.

"Then walk."

He was propelled by the goons up two long flights of clammy steps with his arms behind him. At the top, they moved down a long, wide hall and into an elaborately furnished great room.

Around a table sat three men. Carter recognized two of them. From the uniform, he guessed the third was Brigadier General Jeffrey Cornwall.

There was a delicious, enticing smell of grilled bacon wafting from the table, and the smell of the coffee drew Carter like a magnet.

"Good morning, Carter," General Adrian Dillon said. "Please, sit. Would you care for some breakfast?"

"Just coffee," Carter replied.

He poured himself, and checked out Major General Adrian Dillon over the rim of the cup. The man was dressed in gray worsted slacks and a dark blue turtleneck pullover. He was a deeply tanned, hard-muscled man, slight and wiry, quick-moving and precise, who did everything with a minimum of wasted effort.

His face was sharp-featured, the pale blue eyes very alert, and he smiled easily, as though to put his visitor completely at ease, or perhaps to lull him into a false sense of security.

It was the kind of smile, Carter was thinking, that was not in the least false. But it was nonetheless a trifle devious, as though an overt display of affability might fool a lesser man into betraying the workings of his own mind. Behind it, he was sure, there was a knife-edged sharpness that was absolutely deadly.

"Wynne I think you know."

Carter smiled at the bandaged man. "How's the nose?"

Wynne started to come out of his chair, but the general's hand halted him. "And the gentleman to my right is General Cornwall."

Carter nodded, and Cornwall got right to it. "What the hell is your agency, Carter? We can't find you anywhere."

The Killmaster poured a second cup. "I'm freelance."

"Bullshit!" Wynne shouted.

"Gentlemen." Dillon held up his palms for calm. "That's not really the point right now anyway, Jeff. Look here, Carter, you've gotten your nose in a big operation . . . one years in the making."

"And one doomed to defeat, General."

"Those are the words of an adversary, Carter. What we need to know from you are the names of your superiors, the people you have been reporting to. At this stage, I doubt if anyone would listen to them, but we can't afford too much speculation for at least a few more days."

"What have you done with Trilby Royce?" Carter growled.

Cornwall jumped in. "She is in one of the tower bedrooms. She hasn't been harmed."

"No," Carter replied, "I don't suppose she has. When you bring off your 'rescue' of Aldami, she'll be identified as one of the kidnappers and have some kind of an 'accident,' right?"

Suddenly, to Carter's surprise, the atmosphere around the table changed. The three men seemed to relax. The conversation shifted to chatter about the building situation in Madagascar. They talked openly about their plans for the next few days in front of him.

Finally the general stood and Carter's three watchdogs came across the room.

"Of course you know, Carter, that you will have to disappear," the general said. "But I don't butcher or mistreat prisoners of war." He turned to the guards. "Take him to the tower bedroom to join the woman, and don't harm him any further unless he deserves it."

"Yes, sir."

Carter was in a daze as they led him from the room. He knew that somehow he had told them exactly what they had wanted to know, but for the life of him he couldn't figure out what it was.

The bedroom in the tower turned out to be a two-room suite with a bath big enough to hold court in. A huge bed with an ornately carved wooden headboard dominated the room. It was strewn with fat pillows set on a coverlet that looked like a captured cloud.

Three steps led from the rich carpet to the bed, giving the suggestion of an altar. A night table set with a myriad of switches stood next to the bed. The ceiling above, and much of the wall space, was mirrored. The glass had a rose tint. There was a fully stocked bar on which cut-glass decanters, each with a gold pendant bearing a label identifying the contents, were ranked. Carter looked the bottles over and decided the world held a lot more potables than he had imagined.

Opening to the left was a large sitting room, opulently furnished in soft, fragrant leather. Paintings that he assumed were worth a lot of money hung on the walls. Here there were no mirrors. In the other direction lay a vast bath with a sunken tub of rose-hued marble, and beyond that was a dressing room. Closets there held racks of clothes obviously intended to fulfill any fantasy—or fetish—that might strike the male or female fancy.

Carter breathed a sigh of relief when he saw their bag on a low stand by the bed.

He was just checking out the contents when the door opened again and a tall blonde came in, followed by Trilby. The blonde smirked and backed out, closing the door behind her.

Trilby looked around. "Well, we who are about to die are going to do it in luxury."

"Are you all right?"

She shook her head. "They never laid a hand on me. You look like hell."

"I'll be okay after a hot soak."

Before she could say anything else, Carter hotfooted it into the bath. He turned both taps on full blast. She stood in the doorway.

"How are we going to use—"

Carter put a finger to her lips and tugged her close to the tub. He pulled her down until they were both on their knees, their heads close to the rushing water. Only then did he put his lips close to her ear and speak.

"There are probably some pads and pens in that desk in the sitting room. Get them."

She nodded her understanding and took off.

Carter checked the rooms. He found bugs everywhere, particularly by the bed and vanity, behind the mirrors in the bath, and near the table in the sitting room.

All of them were cleverly disguised or concealed, and he left them that way.

He still had the nagging feeling that he had told them everything they wanted to know, but he guessed that he and Trilby had been put in the suite together just in case they could get a little bonus through the bugs.

He checked the suitcase and found the two bras intact. Most of the vast array of clothing in the closets bore an assortment of monograms, as did the scarves he unearthed in a drawer. All the monograms were a variation of the initials CSF.

AXE had not unearthed any record of ownership for Castillo Augustine, but Carter guessed that the real owner was Carmen San Filippo.

Back in the bath, he stripped and slipped into the tub. He turned on the jets of the Jacuzzi and made more noise by splashing around. But still he didn't speak. Instead, he took one of the pads and a pen from Tribly, and wrote.

Did they question you?

Not much. They didn't seem to care if I knew anything or not.

I got the impression from the general that we have a couple of days, maybe three. Did they mention Aldami?

No, she wrote, *but I saw him.*

When?

By the pool, with a tall, redheaded woman. She looked Spanish.

Carter nodded. That, he thought, would probably be San Filippo. So the gang's all here.

He scribbled again: *Were there any guards?*

Trilby nodded. *Three, but they seemed to be watching the road more than guarding Aldami.*

Carter mulled this over for a few moments. Then, slowly, he started remembering things.

He wrote again: *Where are the helicopter pads?*

We landed on the roof. The pad is in the middle between this tower and the one over the other wing. I think that's where they are keeping Aldami. The other pad is on the lawn beyond the swimming pool.

Suddenly Carter spoke aloud. "Want to make love?"

She was too surprised and aghast not to speak out loud herself. "What? You're mad!"

Carter chuckled. "We're between a rock and a hard place. We might as well enjoy the time we have left." On the pad he wrote, *Take your clothes off, woman. I want to play with your underwear!*

She got the picture and moved into the bedroom. Carter stepped from the tub and dried himself. After tearing up the slips of paper they had used for conversation, he flushed them away.

Trilby was sitting on the bed in only her panties when he entered the bedroom. He kissed her lightly on the tip of each breast.

"You're not cooperating."

Her eyes rolled into her head as she understood. As she went into her act, Carter went to work on the bras. It took nearly an hour to dismantle them, form the plastique into balls, and use the toilet again to get rid of the lacy remnants.

By that time Trilby was bathed in perspiration and her voice was hoarse from groaning.

She wrote on the pad, *Enough is enough!*

Carter wrote, *Right, but I'll bet you've turned on half the guards!*

She gave him a look that would kill, and headed for the bath and a shower.

Carter dressed and hid the plastique in every conceivable part of his clothing.

Lunch was served by two guards, one pushing a tray and the other holding a machine pistol.

Precisely an hour later, the two men returned and removed the tray, using the same routine.

Carter now knew when he would strike.

As they were leaving, he said, "I want to talk to the general."

"What about?"

"A deal."

The guard laughed. "I don't think he'd be interested."

"I think he would be," Carter replied. "Tell him that Cory Reader managed to send Josh the whole story before she was killed."

It worked. They were back in twenty minutes and leading Carter down the stairs. Twice he managed to falter and plant two plastique pellets. He did the same in the lower hallway.

At the end of the lower hall they mounted a short flight of steps and went through a door that led down a flight of steps into the bowels of the castle. They crossed the basement to a third door, and into a long, downward-sloping tunnel-ramp.

They came out on a catwalk overlooking a wide, deep room filled with computers, telex machines, and communication equipment. Technicians roamed between the banks of machinery. Around the catwalk, Carter noticed other tunnels leading upward.

He knew he was in the brain center of Comrex, and said so.

"Perceptive," Dillon said, lounging on the desk. "Now, what's this crap about Cory Reader?"

"Just that, crap. But I figured it would get me down here to see you."

"All right. Why?"

Carter stood and moved around the office. Neither the guard nor Dillon made a move to stop him. "I do want to make a deal."

The general looked bored. "Go ahead."

"Before I came in, our people made a special deal

with MI6. I suppose you know there's a special British SAS team on Gibraltar."

"I do."

"If I don't signal by ten o'clock tonight that I have Aldami out of here, they do a twenty-two man drop and take this place apart."

It was wild and farfetched, but Carter was banking on Dillon's believing that wild and farfetched was the norm.

He was right. From the look on the general's face, Carter had gotten to him. The Killmaster pressed his advantage.

"You've got eight or ten men here. They may be good, but they're no match for a crack SAS antiterrorist team. Right?"

He was wary, but he was thinking. "You may be right, yes."

"Okay, you've got the intelligence. Put it to work. Check and see if that team is on alert instead of on the usual standby status. If you find out they are, bring me down here again and I send the signal to keep them on Gibraltar."

Dillon crossed around the desk and eased into his leather chair. "You're still quite a pain in the ass, Carter."

"Just my job."

"And if the team is on alert, and I allow you to send the message . . . ?"

"We live," Carter said. "Still in custody, of course. Let's face it, General, once you've got your own country to operate out of, we can't hurt you. And when it comes down to it, we're both on the same side. If I'm going to die, I'd rather have the bad guys kill me."

He followed up his little speech by swallowing deeply and tensing his neck muscles to create sweat on his face.

Dillon was a sharp old bird, but Carter knew he had piqued the man's curiosity. He stared at Carter through the tent of his own fingers for a long time before he spoke.

"Okay, I'll do some checking." He nodded to the guards. "Take him back to the tower."

Carter had planted two of the plastique balls in the office. He managed to lay down four more of them in the computer room as he passed through.

Back in the fancy suite, he moved out onto the balcony for a smoke as Trilby watched anxiously behind him.

The two guards in the garden and on the wall below watched him for a minute or two, and then turned their attention back to the countryside.

Carter let four of the plastique pellets dribble off the edge of the roof. He tossed two more as far as he could into the garden. Another went over the top of the tower. He had four left. When two of these were planted in the suite, he sat down on the bed with Trilby, a pad, and a pen.

We go when they bring dinner, he wrote. *Here's what you do. . . .*

NINETEEN

The stage was set.

The radio by the bed was going strong. Trilby was in the bathroom with the shower running. Carter had muffled all but one mike in the sitting room.

Even the weather was in their favor. Lightning cut across the sky outside and a light rain had started.

They were right on time, and the routine didn't change. Number One came through the door raking the room with the business end of the Ingram. Satisfied that Carter wasn't going to play gorilla and tear him apart with his superspy bare hands, he backed off to stand beside the door. At a vocal signal, Number Two waltzed in with a smile, pushing the trolley.

Carter crossed to the tray and started pulling away napkins and lifting various dishes.

''The general sent a message,'' Number One said.

''Oh?'' Carter replied, pouring a cup of coffee from the server and keeping the lid open with his thumb.

''Yeah, something about Gibraltar,'' he said, practically shouting so he could be heard above the noise in the room. ''He said to tell you that you're full of shit.''

"Interesting," Carter replied, shouting himself. "I'll relay that to my comrade-in-arms: Trilby!"

She made a royal entrance through the bathroom door, slamming it behind her. She looked absolutely innocent in her stark nudity. The effect on the two guards was instantaneous.

"Jesus Christ," gasped the tray pusher.

The one with the Ingram didn't say a word. He just gaped, and the muzzle of the machine pistol dropped just enough.

Carter nailed him in the face with the rest of the hot coffee in the pot. At the same time, Trilby went for Number Two, nailing him right in the crotch with the side of her foot.

Carter chopped Number One on the wrist, and the Ingram fell to the floor. The man tried to recover, but the Killmaster got both his knees with vicious kicks. As he went down, Carter broke his neck with another vicious kick.

Trilby was holding her own, but it was only a matter of time. Carter grabbed the Ingram and split the back of his skull.

"You all right?" he asked.

"I think so," she said, hopping gingerly on one foot. "But I might have broken a toe."

"Live with it. Get dressed and let's get out of here."

In seconds she was dressed in slacks, a jacket, and a pair of boots. While she dressed, Carter relieved the trolley pusher of a .38 revolver. Number One had an Army-issue Colt in his belt. Carter did a number on the clip, left one shell in the chamber, and stuck the .45 in his belt.

"Ready?" he said, turning to Trilby.

"As much as I'll ever be."

He shoved the .38 in her hand. "Can you use this?"

With one hand she flipped the cylinder open, twirled it, and flipped it closed. "You bet your ass."

"Good. Follow my lead no matter what happens."

"I'm sticking to you like the proverbial glue," she whispered, and they closed the door softly behind them.

They went down to a pair of glass doors and out onto the roof. It was raining harder now, but the thunder and lightning had let up.

About a hundred yards away, they could see the lights in the other tower, and a pair of glass doors and a hallway similar to the one they had just exited.

Halfway there was one of the two choppers. Carter stopped beside the machine and used the footholds to climb up over the bubble to the rotor shaft.

He attached one of the two plastique pellets he had left to the rotor shaft, and dropped back to the roof.

"You've got your transmitter, haven't you?" he asked.

Trilby patted her jacket pocket. "Right here."

"Okay. Yours controls the charge I just put on that chopper. For God's sake, don't snap it and activate unless I tell you to."

She nodded and they ran for the glass doors. In the hall, Carter slowed. At the door, he gently turned the knob and smiled.

It was unlocked.

He went into the room tugging the .45 from his belt.

Bevello Aldami was at the window in a dressing gown, staring down at the garden in the rain. Carmen San Filippo was lying on the bed in a negligee and reading a book.

As Carter came through the door, Aldami whirled in shock. Carmen San Filippo dropped her book and dived for a Beretta on the night table.

She was just bringing it up when Carter fired the chamberred slug in the .45 between her breasts. The impact drove her up against the headboard and she rolled to the floor.

"Bevello Aldami?" Carter asked, as if he didn't know.

"Yes . . . who are you . . . ?"

"Never mind that," the Killmaster said. "C'mon, we're getting you out of here. Trilby, cover the rear!"

They moved into the hall and down to the main floor without any interference.

"Do you know the way to the helicopter pad from here?"

"Yes," Aldami answered.

"You lead her," Carter said. "I'll catch up. Here, you might need this." He reversed the .45 and slapped it into Aldami's hand.

Carter watched them go through the doors and into the gardens. Just before they reached the wall, Trilby took Aldami's hand and tugged him down behind the safety of the tall garden wall.

Good girl, Carter thought, *follows every order.*

He took the transmitter from his own pocket and placed it on the floor. Then he gently cracked it under his heel until he heard the glass crack.

It would take ten seconds.

He dived into the garden and took up a place by some trees on the inner side of the swimming pool.

Aloud, he counted, "Eight . . . nine . . . ten . . ."

All hell broke loose above and behind him.

He paid no attention. He brought the muzzle of the Ingram up and waited.

It didn't take long.

They came roaring through the patio gate, all three of them.

Carter stepped from the trees and let the Ingram chatter. He cut a swath across the front, nailing all three of them with one burst.

They hadn't hit the concrete before he was at the door leading down to the control center. Halfway down the tunnel, he met another guard.

He flipped the Ingram to semi-auto, and spread the man open with a short three-pull burst.

The communications center was a mess and there was fire. As Carter bolted through the door, two technicians spotted him. The Killmaster lowered his shoulder, driving one into the other.

They went down.

They weren't armed, so Carter left them and ran on to the office.

Jeffrey Cornwall was on the floor by the desk. There was a gaping hold in his side pumping blood like a faucet, but he was still alive.

Carter stood over him with the Ingram. "Cornwall . . . ?" When he didn't answer, Carter slapped him. The eyes fluttered open. "Cornwall!"

"You . . . what happened . . . ?" the man sputtered.

"Where's the general?" the Killmaster hissed.

"I don't know."

"Wynne?"

"Around, somewhere," he gasped, and blood trickled from the corner of his lips.

"Do you know the combination to that safe?"

"No."

"You don't know shit, do you, Cornwall."

"Go to hell."

Carter shot him once, in the forehead, and mashed the last plastique pellet against the combination dial on the safe.

It was automatic now, since the transmitter he had activated topside was still sending. He jammed a coil of detonator wire into the mass and ran for the other room, counting.

It blew on ten precisely, and Carter was up and running back.

The door to the safe was hanging open by one hinge. He pawed through the contents . . . money, papers, computer printouts . . . until he spotted some microfilm. It was in a small box marked MADRAS ACCOUNTS.

There were four of them. He jammed them into his pockets and took off for the second floor.

In the garden, a few white-coated technicians were running around wildly, but once again none of them was armed.

Carter spotted Trilby standing by the chopper. Aldami was just behind her left shoulder.

Carter ran. "Get in! Get in the chopper!"

Neither one of them moved. Just as Carter reached them, Aldami's hand came around the girl's shoulder and ground the muzzle of the .45 into her ear.

"Drop it, Carter."

"Well, well," Carter said, coming to a halt less than two feet from them. "So *you* are the brains."

Aldami smiled. "And most of the money. Drop it or I'll put her pretty brains all over the garden."

"I don't think so," Carter growled.

As he stepped forward, pulling his hand from his pocket, Aldami fired. The hammer of the .45 merely clicked.

"I didn't think you knew shit about guns, Aldami."

Carter opened his hand to show the other man that it was full of .45 cartridges.

Aldami pushed Trilby to the side, but he didn't go anywhere himself. Carter clipped him on the jaw with the butt of the Ingram.

Before his knees hit the ground, Carter had him under the armpits and was hoisting him into the chopper.

"Get in," he told Trilby, "and put a belt around him. We want him well and alive!"

She did as she was told, no questions asked, as Carter pulled himself into the left-hand seat.

He fired up the engine and engaged the rotors until they were humming.

"You ready?" he shouted over the roar.

Trilby nodded and Carter lifted. He tipped the nose forward and tilted out over the road and the vineyards. About a mile out, he arced around and headed east, toward Spain.

Over his left shoulder he saw the other chopper lift off the roof pad.

"He turned on me at the chooper," Trilby said, "Surprised me."

"I figured he would," Carter said. "That's why I emptied the clip in the forty-five."

"But how did you know?"

"Lots of things, little things. When I talked to Dillon, Wynne, and Cornwall, they asked me some questions, but they wanted some different answers. When I intimated to them that I still thought Aldami was a kidnap victim, they were relieved. Also, one thing has bothered me all along. Once they took over in Aldami's country, they really had nothing. Aldami couldn't control his people if they thought the Americans were running him."

"So he really did want power?"

Carter nodded. "And in exchange, he and the general would expand together into the rest of Africa."

Out of the side mirror now, Carter could see the other chopper coming up fast.

In the rear seat behind them, Aldami came awake and struggled against his safety harness.

"Check him," Carter said.

Trilby touched the pulse on his neck. "He's all right, but I think his jaw is broken."

"That's okay," Carter said. "If he can't talk, he can write, and I think I've got compound evidence." He patted the pocket containing the microfilm.

He dropped over a mesa of vineyards, and suddenly the pursuit ship was right behind them.

Something rattled hard.

"What was that?" Trilby exclaimed.

"The other chopper is armed," Carter growled. "They have a pair of 7.62s. They just put a burst across our nose."

He dropped a little, and banked to his right. The ground careened toward them, filling the windshield, and Carter pulled the aircraft up again, banking left, going over the crest with less than a yard to spare.

"Shit!" Trilby screamed, slamming back in her seat.

"Hold on!" Carter shouted as they blasted across the top of a hill, then into the open sky, dropping twenty feet like a rock to get the hill between them and the other helicopter.

"I'll make you a deal," she yelled.

"What?"

"You keep it in the air and I'll hold on."

He nodded.

Behind them, the helicopter came over the edge of the

mesa. Carter waited a beat, then shifted left. A moment later, he heard the rattle of the 7.62 mini-gun.

He switched his lights on, then tapped the foot pedals slightly, weaving the tail boom, and pulled the collective again, lifting them up.

"What the hell are you doing?" Trilby shrieked.

"The light on our tail," Carter explained. "It's what his eye automatically goes to. When I shift it, it throws his line of sight off."

They raced over another low hill, and in the distance Carter could see the outline of a huge, wide gorge.

The pursuit ship fired, ripping the air under them.

Carter raised and banked left. "Goddammit, we could do this all night long."

"I'd rather not," Trilby choked.

"Same here."

Carter lowered the chopper, slanting in toward the canyon, blasting over the edge, and dropping into it.

The pursuit ship followed, opening up again.

Carter banked away, turning across the canyon. A grove of willows rushed under them, then a column of rock. He dropped the chopper down, slowing it slightly.

Trilby felt it, and looked at the air-speed indicator. The needle dropped more.

"He'll catch us!"

"I know," Carter said.

He surged up over another line of trees and eased down them, turning up a creek, staying about six feet off the water.

The other helicopter followed, closing in on them.

Dark, shadowed banks streaked up around them. Carter blasted through a narrow opening and jerked a hard left around a turn, then brought his chopper farther left, screaming up and over the trees on the edge of the water and coming back around 180 degrees, over the top of the turn they'd just come out of.

"Okay, you dumb bastard," he hissed, "you can't say I didn't try to save your ass."

"What does that mean?" she asked.

"You'll see."

Just then, the other chopper came roaring up from the trees and the radio came to life.

"Carter, this is Dillon. Can you hear me, Carter?"

They were just below and to the left. Carter could see Wynne's bruised face through the bubble. The general was in the other seat with the hand mike.

"Carter, I know you can hear me. Get on your radio! You're going to kill us all flying in this weather!"

Carter reached for the mike. "*Que sera, sera,* General."

"Set it down, Carter! Give me back Aldami and you've got your deal!"

"No deals, General. I've got your money and your power. You've got nothing left to bargain with."

"That's where you're wrong, my boy. Somewhere there's another Aldami. Now, set it down or we'll blow you out of the sky!"

Carter turned in the seat. Aldami was awake now, and he must have heard every word. His dark face was too shades lighter and his eyes were pure white.

"Hear that, old chap?" Carter hooted. "You're expendable! What do you say? Want to work a deal with our State Department? Our country had nothing to do with kidnapping you, right? Person or persons unknown, right?"

The radio came on again. "We're falling back, Carter. Give me an answer or we'll put a burst right into you."

The other chopper slipped back and took a position about fifty yards above and behind them.

"Did you hear that?" Carter yelled. "I do think the general means it. You'd better talk to me, or I start saying my own prayers."

The head started nodding. "Yes, yes, anything you say."

"Trilby, the transmitter. Put it under your heel and get ready."

She took the transmitter from her pocket and sat staring at it in her palm.

"Trilby, do it!"

With a small sob, she leaned forward and placed the capsule under her left heel.

"Carter . . . ?"

"Yes, General, may you roast in hell."

"You dumb bastard."

"Now!" Carter shouted, and slammed the collective stick down, and hauled the cyclic stick back toward him, zeroing the helicopter out. They dropped like a rock, straight down.

Trilby screamed.

Carter jammed the right pedal down, spinning them around.

The other chopper roared over them, and Carter pulled the collective up, and the cyclic out, catching their chopper in midair, slamming him and Trilby hard.

The impact threw Trilby to one side, straining at her seat belt and screaming. Carter pulled the copter up, gaining power, angling away from the other aircraft.

"Did you do it?" Carter shouted.

"No, no, I can't!"

"Trilby, your old man was an asshole, but he was your

old man." He reached over, gripped her ankle, and jammed down. He could feel rather than hear the glass break under her heel.

The other helicopter banked slightly, then suddenly blossomed orange, exploding, filling the sky with flames.

Carter laid the chopper hard to the left, skirting through the edge of the explosion.

Then the other helicopter was gone, just glowing streaks in the sky.

Carter eased around, heading back toward the east and Spain.

Bevello Aldami gurgled from the rear. "You . . . you knew you could win all the time!"

Carter smiled. "I sure did. It's scum like you, Aldami, who keep me in business. But it's people like the general who are really dangerous."

He glanced over at Trilby. Her face was chalk white and she was staring straight ahead without blinking.

"Ms. Royce, have you ever seen the sunset from the beaches just north of Acapulco?"

"N-No, I don't believe I have."

Carter chuckled. "You will, soon."

DON'T MISS THE NEXT NEW NICK CARTER SPY THRILLER

THE KOREAN KILL

"Jacques Bonner and someone called Dr. Kwon."

Hun Wook leaned forward and placed his elbows on the table. "What do you hope to accomplish, Mr. Crider?"

"I want to collect two hundred and fifty thousand dollars that is owed to me. If you act as my introduction to Bonner, ten percent is yours."

Carter could sense from the man's smile that he thought Carter was an idiot. But that was all right. Wook would contact Bonner, and there was an outside chance that he would be able to get inside the casino through the front door.

There were chances, of course, that several other things could happen, but Carter had prepared himself for everything.

"For such a sum of money, Mr. Crider, I will most certainly see what I can do. Excuse me for a few moments, if you will."

The few moments turned into nearly an hour before he returned to the office, beaming. "Mr. Bonner will be most happy to sit down and talk with you. The Empire Casino is located in the Nampo-dong amusement area. The address is on this paper. Any taxi driver can take you there."

Carter stood. "We will be in touch."

"I sincerely hope so, sir."

Again Carter took the limp hand, and left the office. At the edge of Texas Town, he bypassed two taxis who cruised him, and caught a third.

"Yes, sir?"

"This address," Carter said, and showed the man the paper that Wook had given him.

The driver shrugged and dropped the flag. "Very much traffic tonight. Better to take smaller streets. All right with you, sir?"

"Whatever," Carter said.

They drove for about twenty minutes before the traffic thinned to a trickle so Carter could spot the tail. It was an older model Renault sedan.

They were on a quiet side street now, the driver avoiding the heavy traffic of the boulevard that paralleled them. Carter turned and looked out the rear window again, and saw the black Renault sedan only a half block behind them and closing.

"How long has that car been behind us?" he said to the driver.

"Sir?"

"The car!" Carter snapped. "Behind us!"

The driver glanced in the rearview mirror. "Ah. Yes, a car."

Carter made an ugly sound in his throat and curled the fingers of his left hand around the back of the driver's neck. "You son of a bitch, you're with 'em, aren't you!"

"I don't know what you say."

"I'm no expert on Pusan, but I think the Nampo-dong amusement area is about eight miles in the other direction."

Now the driver was visibly shaken. Carter could feel him shaking clear through his neck, and the collar of his shirt was suddenly soaked through with sweat.

"Turn right at this next corner!" Carter barked, pulling the Luger but keeping it low behind the seat.

The driver glanced again through the rearview mirror at the Renault, his eyes fearful. Carter was sure now that the driver was either one of them or he and several other drivers had been paid to take Carter in a certain direction to a certain place no matter who picked him up.

He flicked off the Luger's safety. It was time to let Jacques Bonner know just how nasty he could get.

The driver was hesitating, weighing his chances of survival with Carter or the occupants of the Renault.

"Turn, you bastard!" Carter ground the muzzle of the Luger in the man's ear to help him to a decision.

The driver made a hard right turn, tires squealing. The driver of the Renault gave up the pretence of holding back, and came around the corner with his own tires screaming.

"Turn left," Carter hissed, "and drive faster!"

He did, and the black car followed, right on their tail. The taxi driver started to accelerate, but the Renault pulled around to the left quickly and came up alongside. Carter could see the faces in the other car, three of them. The driver of the Renault turned hard into the taxi and there was a crashing and rending of metal.

The taxi driver swore and almost lost control of the

cab. It went up onto the curb and barely missed a couple walking on a dusty sidewalk. The driver got control again.

Carter aimed the Luger and fired at the driver of the other car. The Renault bounced and swerved and his aim went wild, but the slug hit the neck of the man riding beside the driver. He jerked limply and then his mouth flew open and he fell onto the driver. The driver pushed him away and crashed again into the taxi. This time the taxi went up over the sidewalk and smashed into a building front and bounced back to the curb, where it slammed into a utility pole.

Carter was thrown into the front seat, where his back and head jammed up against the dash. The taxi driver hit the windshield with his face, but not before the steering wheel had crushed his chest in on his heart and lungs. There was an accompanying explosion of sound, with metal and wood and glass all shrieking under the impact, and then the car was motionless, the radiator hissing steam.

Carter raised his bruised body and aimed the Luger toward the other car, which had pulled to a stop just beyond the utility pole. The two remaining men jumped out and ran in a crouch toward him. He fired off another shot at the closest man and the gunman yelled, his arms flying outward, his legs moving in different directions until he thumped onto the pavement, pooling blood beneath him.

The last man was hobbling. Light from a streetlight bathed his face for a second before he slid behind it for cover.

It was Booja Dok.

"Well, well, Dok," Carter yelled, putting an aching, groaning rasp in his voice, "have you come to peel my skin?"

"Come out of there, and I will not kill you!" Dok

shouted at the shattered windshield that obscured his view of Carter.

Crouched like a leopard in the front seat of the taxi, the Luger held up beside his right temple ready for use, Carter let a hard grin tickle the very edge of his straight-lined mouth.

"Do you hear me?" Dok shouted. "Drop your gun and come out!"

Down the street, several heads had appeared at doorways and were bent curiously in their direction.

"You must be injured! I will give you medical help!" Dok called, air hissing through his teeth.

Carter held the gun down lower. "All right. I'm out of ammunition. My right arm is busted. I'm finished."

"Throw your gun out of the car," Dok said in a hard voice.

Carter had been afraid of that. He glanced quickly around the taxi, and saw a heavy clipboard on the seat beside the dead driver. He picked it up and slipped it out the door on his side, the side away from the utility pole and Dok. It clattered to the pavement and the sound was very like that of a small gun.

Behind the pole, Dok craned his neck to see what Carter had thrown out, but could not. He hesitated, then stepped out from behind the pole and walked carefully to the driver's side of the taxi, the gun held out in front of him. He saw the dead driver, and then Carter's head, where he was crouched on the other side of the car.

"Well. That is very good, very smart. Now get to your feet slowly and—"

Carter raised the Luger in an unhurried way, aimed it carefuly while Dok's eyes changed, and fired. The slug hit Dok just over the heart and pushed him backward away from the window of the car, hitting him like a club and sprawling him in the dusty street.

Carter got out of the cab and came around into the street to have a look. Dok was all twisted up on the cobbled pavement, the gun still in his hand. His gun hand twitched once, but he was dead.

Quickly, Carter darted from body to body. He collected everything from their pockets and rolled it up in the taxi driver's jacket.

Within two minutes after killing Dok, he was running as hard as he could down a side street toward a sign that said Underground in Korean.

He took the first train two stops, and came back up to street level. He walked a block and darted into a fish market that was just closing.

The old woman in the market thought he was crazy paying a thousand won for a plastic bag.

Back on the street, he dumped the contents of the jacket into the plastic bag and discarded the jacket in a street waste recepticle..

Three blocks farther on, he found another taxi and showed him the address on the paper.

"I know this address is in the Nampo-dong area, he hissed. "If you do not take me directly to the Nampo-dong area, I will pound your ass so far through that seat it will be dragging on the street. Do you understand?"

"*Ye*," the driver said, and dropped the meter with a look at Carter that said, *You are a crazy man!*

—From THE KOREAN KILL
A New Nick Carter Spy Thriller
From Jove in April 1989

NICK
CARTER